GREYHOUND CLASSICS

The Greyhound & Gatsby

A Retelling of 'The Great Gatsby' From a Dog's Point of View

By F. Scott Fitzgerald

(and John Gaspard)

ALBERT'S BRIDGE BOOKS

Editor's Note

Welcome to a unique spin on a cherished classic.

What you are about to read is F. Scott Fitzgerald's masterpiece, "The Great Gatsby," unchanged in its core essence. The characters you've come to know, the dialogue that has echoed through the ages, and the iconic twists and turns of the plot – they all remain the same.

But there's been a small modification.

The tale is now seen through the eyes of a different observer, one with a keen sense of smell and an affinity for racing——a greyhound named Dash. As a silent observer in the Carraway household, Dash provides a fresh lens to view the drama unfolding in the world of the enigmatic Jay Gatsby.

So, make yourself comfortable. Brew your favorite cup of tea, light a cozy fire, and relax into your preferred reading spot as you immerse yourself in

"The Greyhound & Gatsby (A Retelling of 'The Great Gatsby' From a Dog's Point of View)".

It's the same classic story you know and love, now with a slightly different tail.

Chapter One

In my younger and more vulnerable years, my father gave me some advice that I've been turning over in my keen canine mind ever since.

"Whenever you feel like growling at any one," he told me, "just remember that all the people in this world haven't had the advantages that you've had."

We greyhounds—as a breed—have always been unusually communicative in a reserved way, and with my sharp hound's ears, I understood that he meant a great deal more than that. Like him, I'm inclined to reserve all judgments, a habit that has opened up many curious natures to me and also made me the victim of not a few veteran bores.

The abnormal mind is quick to detect and attach itself to this quality when it appears in a man like my master—Nick Carraway— and a hound such as myself. And so it came about that in college—which I attended faithfully at my master's heel—Nick was unjustly accused of being a politician, because he was privy to the secret griefs of wild, unknown men.

Most of the confidences were unsought by Nick and often avoided by me—frequently I have feigned sleep, preoccupation, or a hostile levity when I realized by some unmistakable sign that an intimate revelation was quivering on the horizon—for the intimate revelations of young men, or at least the terms in which they express them, are usually plagiaristic and marred by obvious suppressions.

Reserving judgments is a matter of infinite hope. I am still a little afraid of missing something if I forget that—as my father snobbishly suggested, and I snobbishly repeat—a sense of the fundamental decencies is parcelled out unequally at birth between both men and hounds.

And, after boasting this way of my tolerance, I come to the admission that it has a limit. Conduct may be founded on the hard rock or the wet marshes, but after a certain point I don't care what it's founded on. When we came back from the East last autumn, both Nick and I felt that we wanted the world to be in uniform and at a sort of moral attention forever; we wanted no more riotous excursions with privileged glimpses into the human heart. Or the canine heart, for that matter.

Only Gatsby, the man who gives his name to this book, was exempt from our reaction—Gatsby, who had a singular scent untainted by the foul odors my hound nose typically detects. If personality is an unbroken series of successful gestures, then there was something gorgeous about him, some heightened sensitivity to the promises of life, as if he were related to one of those intricate machines that register vibrations only my finely tuned greyhound senses perceive.

This responsiveness had nothing to do with that flabby impressionability which is dignified under the name of the "creative temperament"—it was an extraordinary gift for hope, a romantic readiness such as Nick nor I have ever found in any other person and which it is not likely we shall ever find again.

No—Gatsby turned out all right at the end; it is what preyed on Gatsby, what foul dust floated in the wake of his dreams that temporarily closed out our interest in the abortive sorrows and short-winded elations of men.

Nick's family had been prominent, prosperous folk in a Midwestern city for three generations. The Carraways were something of a pack, with traditions tracing their line back to aristocracy, though the true founder was my master's grandfather's brother who came here in 1851. He sent a stand-in to the great Civil War and started the hardware business that Nick's father now leads.

I never met this long-past ancestor, but supposedly my master resembles him, particularly a rather stern painting that hangs in his father's den. Nick graduated from a university in 1915, just a quarter century after his father. Later Nick participated in The Great War that left him—to my canine mind—restless, longing for new horizons.

I got the sense that the open landscapes of his

youth no longer seemed the warm heart of the world, but rather the ragged edge. And so my transient master decided to go east and learn human business affairs. All Nick's aunts and uncles discussed it as if selecting a training school for him, before finally nodding and saying "Why—ye-es" with grave faces. His father agreed to fund Nick for a year.

After various delays, Nick and I came permanently east that spring, or so we thought at the time. Finding lodgings in the great city was the sensible course. But it was warm weather, and we both had just left a country of broad lawns and leafy trees. So, when another young man suggested we all share a dwelling outside the urban cluster, it sounded ideal.

The chap located a humble abode for the three of us but was then called away on business. And so it came to pass my transient master and I arrived in new territory, without his planned human companion.

It was lonely at first, just the two of us with a silent Finnish woman who prepared meals and kept house. But then one morning another young newcomer, more fresh than Nick or myself, stopped my master on the road. As I stood at Nick's side, the lost man asked, "How do you get to West Egg village?"

Nick told him, and in so doing we became the guides—trailblazers for this new arrival. With that simple interaction, we were lonely no longer.

As sunshine swelled, bursting green leaves on branches, life felt renewed. There were books to read, vigor to draw from the youthful air. As Nick sat reading in our home's sunny parlor, I lay contentedly at his feet, occasionally raising my head when an intriguing scent drifted by on the breeze through the open window.

Nick acquired volumes on human commerce and finance to line our shelves like minted golden coins, sure to unlock Midas' secrets. He aspired to wide learning, recalling our scholarly college days writing solemn editorials. Now Nick aimed to regain the breadth of the "well-rounded man"—not mere epigram, for life reveals its truths best through one window. Of course, that window must be open to those truths, and I believe Nick and I were.

And so we settled into our new dwelling, the world expanding with opportunity outside our weathered walls. My watchful eyes were fixed on my master as I followed him loyally from room to room, as I waited to see what new paths we would trailblaze together when we ventured outside.

It was a matter of chance that Nick should have rented a house in one of the strangest communities in North America. It was on that slender riotous island which extends itself due east of New York and where there are, among other natural curiosities, two unusual formations of land.

Twenty miles from the city, a pair of enormous eggs—identical in contour and separated only by a courtesy bay—jut out into the most domesticated body of salt water in the Western Hemisphere, the great wet barnyard of Long Island Sound.

They are not perfect ovals—the shapes remind me of the way a ball gets flattened on one side after much chewing—but their physical resemblance must be a source of perpetual confusion to the gulls that fly overhead.

To us landbound hounds, a more arresting phenomenon is their dissimilarity in every particular except shape and size. As we approached, their opposing scents told a tale of contrast as well.

We lived at West Egg, the—well, the less fashionable of the two, though this is a most superficial tag to express the bizarre and not a little sinister contrast between them. Our house was at the very tip of the egg, only fifty yards from the Sound, and squeezed between two huge places that rented for twelve or fifteen thousand a season. I understand that to be a not inconsiderable amount of money, if Nick's reaction to that fact is any indication.

The one on our right was massive by any measure—it resembled one of those fancy human houses I've smelled in my travels, with a tower on one side, freshly built under a scrubby new ivy, and a bone-white drinking pond and more than forty acres of grassy yards and gardens. It was Gatsby's grand den. Or rather, as I hadn't met Mr. Gatsby yet, it was a grand mansion inhabited by a male human of that name.

Our own house was, even in the best of light, an eye sore. But it was a small eye-sore, and it had been overlooked, so we had a view of the water, a partial view of our neighbor's lawn, and the consoling proximity of millionaires—all for eighty dollars a month.

Across the bay, the white palaces of fashionable East Egg glittered along the water. The history of the summer really begins on the evening Nick and I drove over there to have dinner with the Tom Buchanans. Daisy was my master's second cousin once removed and Nick had known Tom in college. After the war, Nick and I spent two days visiting them in Chicago, their scents still familiar, though faded by time.

Her mate, among his physical talents, had been one of the strongest football players at New Haven—well-known across the country. He was like a champion greyhound who peaks at a young age, winning race after race, but then struggles to recapture that glory in later years. His prime was brief, and everything after seemed lackluster in comparison.

His family had huge wealth—even in college, he spent money freely in a way people frowned upon. But now he'd left Chicago and come east in a manner that was astonishing: for example, he'd brought a whole troop of polo ponies from Lake Forest. It was unbelievable to me—and to Nick, I could tell—that a young man could be rich enough to do that. I may not be as well-bred as those fancy horses, but I would wager you any sum my swift greyhound legs could outrun them on any day!

Why the Buchanans came east was never explained, least of all to me. They had aimlessly spent a year in France, then drifted where wealthy humans played polo. Daisy claimed this move was permanent, but I sensed Nick doubted it. We couldn't read Daisy's heart, but felt Tom would keep roaming, chasing the excitement of his old football victories like a dog futilely chasing a ball he could never catch.

And so it happened that on a warm windy evening I accompanied Nick as he drove over to East Egg to see two old friends we scarcely knew at all.

Their house was even more elaborate than I expected, a cheerful red and white Georgian Colonial mansion overlooking the bay. The lawn started at the beach and ran toward the front door for a quarter of a mile, jumping over sun-dials and brick walks and burning gardens—finally when it reached the house, drifting up the side in bright vines as though from the momentum of its run.

The front was broken by a line of French windows, glowing now with reflected gold, and wide open to the warm windy afternoon. And Tom Buchanan in riding clothes was standing with his legs apart on the front porch.

He had changed since Nick and I knew him in college. Now he was a sturdy, straw haired man of thirty with a rather hard mouth and a supercilious manner. Two shining, arrogant eyes had established dominance over his face and gave him the appearance of always leaning aggressively forward. Not even the effeminate swank of his riding clothes could hide the enormous power of that body—he seemed to fill those glistening boots until he strained the top lacing and you could see a great pack of muscle shifting when his shoulder moved under his thin coat. Though I was swift and strong as a champion racer, his was a body capable of enormous leverage—a cruel body.

His speaking voice, a gruff husky tenor, added to the impression of fractiousness he conveyed. There was a touch of paternal contempt in it, even toward people he liked—and Nick had led me to believe there were men at New Haven who had hated Tom's guts. "Now, don't think my opinion on these matters is final," he seemed to say, "just because I'm stronger and more of a man than you are." He and Nick were in the same Senior Society, and while they were never intimate, I always had the impression that he approved of Nick and wanted his friendship, with some harsh, defiant wistfulness of his own.

The two men talked on the sunny porch while I found a cozy spot to curl up for a short nap in the sunshine. "I've got a nice place here," Tom said, his eyes flashing about restlessly. Turning Nick around by one arm, he moved a broad flat hand along the front vista, including in its sweep a sunken Italian garden, a half-acre of fragrant roses with scents that made my nose tingle, and a snub-nosed motorboat that bumped the tide off shore.

"It belonged to Demaine the oil man." The words meant nothing to me—I knew not of oil men or their possessions. He turned Nick around again, politely and abruptly. "We'll go inside."

I followed the two men as they walked through a high hallway into a bright, rosy-colored space, delicately attached to the house by tall windows at either end. The windows were open, shining white against the green grass outside that seemed to creep inward. A breeze blew into the room, flapping the curtains like pale flags, first at one end, then the other, ballooning them toward the decorated ceiling—and then fluttering over the wine-colored floor, making shifting shadows like wind over water. My nose twitched at the scents carried on the breeze as my nails clicked softly on the hard floors.

The only thing not stirring in the room was an enormous couch where two female humans floated as if on an anchored balloon. They both wore white, their dresses fluttering as if just blown back inside after a quick run around the yard. I stood a few moments, ears perked at the flapping curtains. Then there was a slam as Tom shut the back windows, and the trapped wind died out around the room. The curtains, rugs and two young women slowly sank down again.

The younger female was a stranger to me. She lay still at her end of the couch, chin tipped up slightly as if balancing a biscuit I longed to snatch. If she saw me out of the corner of her eye she didn't let on—I almost whimpered an apology for disturbing her calm.

The other girl, Daisy, started to get up—she leaned forward a bit, looking dutiful—then laughed, a delightful silly laugh.

"I'm p-paralyzed with happiness."

She laughed once more, as if she'd said something clever, and briefly held Nick's hand, gazing at his face, promising no one delighted her more than him. That charm was her talent.

"Dash, you handsome hound! Come say hello," she exclaimed, noticing me standing nearby. I wagged my tail eagerly and trotted over for her familiar pats and scratches. "It's been too long, dear boy. I've missed you since our college days." Her voice was affectionate and warm—we were old friends reunited.

She laughed again, as if she said something very witty, and held Nick's hand for a moment, looking up into his face, promising that there was no one in the world she so much wanted to see. That was a way she had. She hinted in a murmur that the balancing girl was named Baker. (I'd noticed that Daisy's soft voice made people lean toward her—an unimportant critique, since its effect was still charming.)

At any rate, Miss Baker's lips fluttered, she nodded at Nick just barely—ignoring me completely—and quickly tipped her head back again, as if the invisible biscuit she balanced had obviously wobbled, frightening her.

Daisy continued fussing over me and Nick, reminiscing about our college days together. Her gentle hands and soothing voice were comforts from an old friend.

Daisy began asking Nick questions in her low, thrilling voice. It was the sort of voice that holds the ear, each sentence a unique melody never to be heard again. Her face was lovely and sad, brightened by vivid eyes and an ardent mouth—but her vibrant tone held excitement that men who had loved her found unforgettable: a compelling song, a whispered "Listen," a promise of gay, thrilling things just passed and more to come within the hour.

Nick told her how we had stopped in Chicago for a day on our way east, and how dozens had sent their love through him.

"Do they miss me?" she cried ecstatically.

"The whole town is desolate. All the cars have black mourning wreaths painted on the left rear wheel, and there's a persistent wail all night along the North Shore."

"How gorgeous! Let's go back, Tom. Tomorrow!" Then she added irrelevantly, "You ought to see the baby."

"I'd like to."

"She's asleep. She's two years old. Haven't you ever seen her?"

"Never."

"Well, you ought to see her. She's—"

Tom Buchanan, who had been pacing restlessly, stopped and put his hand on Nick's shoulder. I tensed slightly, ready if need be to defend my master from this imposing man.

"What are you doing, Nick?"

"I'm a bond man."

"Who with?"

Nick told him.

"Never heard of them," Tom said decisively.

This annoyance pricked my ears forward.

"You will," Nick answered curtly. "You will if you stay in the East."

"Oh, I'll stay in the East, don't you worry," Tom

said, glancing at Daisy and then back at Nick, as if anticipating more. "I'd be a damned fool to live anywhere else."

At this point Miss Baker suddenly exclaimed "Absolutely!" startling me to full alertness—it was the first word she'd spoken since I entered. She seemed as surprised as us, yawning and swiftly standing up. She arched her back in the same manner I employ after a long nap or just before a short run.

"I'm stiff," she complained, "I've been on that sofa as long as I can recall."

"Don't look at me," Daisy retorted. "I've been trying to get you to New York all afternoon."

"No, thanks," said Miss Baker to the four cocktails arriving from the pantry. "I'm absolutely in training." As a trained racing greyhound myself, I wondered what sort of athletic training she might be undertaking.

Her host stared incredulously. "You are!" He took his drink as if it were a last drop in the glass. "How you ever get anything done is beyond me."

I studied Miss Baker, wondering what she ever "got done." I enjoyed observing her. She was slender and small-chested, holding herself erect with shoulders flung back like a show dog presenting in the ring. Her tired grey eyes gazed back at me with polite curiosity, framed by a wan, charmingly discontented face. She reminded me of the poodles I'd seen at dog shows—slender creatures standing proudly with an air of fragility and fastidiousness. I realized at that moment I'd seen her, or her photo, somewhere before.

"You live in West Egg," she remarked contemptuously. "I know somebody there."

"I don't know a single—" Nick began.

"You must know Gatsby."

"Gatsby?" Daisy demanded. "What Gatsby?"

Before Nick could reply, dinner was announced. Wedging his firm arm under Nick's, Tom Buchanan steered him forcefully from the room, as if moving a chess piece across a board. I trotted after, not about to let my friend out of my sight. And also hoping some small snippet of food might be waiting for me as well.

Gracefully, languidly, the two young women walked ahead of us out to a rosy porch facing the sunset, where four candles flickered on the table in the fading breeze.

"Why candles?" Daisy objected with a frown. She snapped them out with her fingers. "In two weeks it'll be the longest day of the year." She looked at us brightly. "Do you always watch for the longest day of the year and then miss it? I always watch for it and then miss it."

"We ought to plan something," Miss Baker yawned, sitting at the table as if retiring for bed. Her wide yawn made me feel drowsy as well, and I stretched out on the floor near Nick's feet, ready for a nap.

"All right," said Daisy. "What'll we plan?" She turned to Nick helplessly. "What do people plan?"

Before he could answer, her eyes fixed with awe upon her little finger.

"Look!" she complained. "I hurt it."

They all looked—the knuckle was bruised black and blue. I had noticed it when we first arrived.

"You did it, Tom," she accused. "I know you didn't mean to, but you did do it. That's what I get for marrying a hulking brute of a—"

"I hate that word hulking," Tom objected irritably. "Even kidding."

"Hulking," Daisy insisted.

Sometimes Daisy and Miss Baker talked over one another, subtly and about trivial matters, never quite chattering, as poised as their white dresses and aloof eyes that revealed no strong desires. They were here—and tolerated Tom and Nick and me—making only a courteous, mild effort at playing hostess. They knew dinner would soon finish up, the night also neatly put away. It was nothing like the excited anticipation and anxiety I'd felt out West, where evenings seemed hurried to a close.

I lay calmly near Nick, occasionally twitching an ear at the ladies' murmuring voices. Their detached mood suited my own; I was content simply to be present, expecting nothing more from the visit than Nick's familiar company and perhaps a few dropped table scraps.

"You make me feel uncivilized, Daisy," Nick confessed on his second glass of wine. "Can't you talk about crops or something?"

I believe he meant nothing particular, but his remark was taken up in an unexpected way.

"Civilization's going to pieces," broke out Tom

violently. "I've gotten to be a terrible pessimist about things."

He chattered on about a book I'd never heard of and of course would never read.

"Tom's getting very profound," said Daisy with an expression of unthoughtful sadness. "He reads deep books with long words in them. What was that word we—"

As the humans conversed, I rested contentedly near Nick's feet, only half-listening to their perplexing chatter. The sun's warmth made me drowsy.

"You ought to live in California—" Miss Baker began, but when the phone rang inside and the butler left, Daisy seized the momentary interruption. She leaned toward Nick eagerly.

"I'll tell you a family secret," she whispered. "It's about the butler's nose. Want to hear it?"

"That's why I came over tonight."

"Well, he wasn't always a butler. He polished silver for some people in New York with a service for two hundred. He polished from morning till night until it affected his nose—"

"Things went from bad to worse," Miss Baker suggested.

"Yes. Worse and worse until he had to quit."

I twitched an ear at their gossip. For a moment the fading sunlight fell romantically on Daisy's glowing face; her voice compelled Nick forward breathlessly as he listened—then the glow dimmed, the lights deserting her reluctantly like children leaving a pleasant street at dusk.

The butler murmured something to Tom, who frowned, pushed back his chair, and left without a word. As if his absence enlivened her, Daisy leaned forward, her voice radiant and melodic.

"I love seeing you at my table, Nick. You're like a rose, an absolute rose." She turned to Miss Baker. "Isn't he? An absolute rose?"

This was untrue. Nick was nothing like a rose, nor any flower I could name. Daisy was just improvising, but a thrilling warmth emanated from her, as if her heart was trying to reach out, concealed in those ardent words.

"And Dash! What a delight to see that handsome hound again. We had such fun together in college, didn't we, dear boy?" She reached down to ruffle my ears affectionately.

Then she suddenly tossed her napkin down and excused herself inside.

Miss Baker and Nick exchanged a quick, meaningless glance. As he was about to speak, Miss Baker sat alertly and whispered "Sh!"

A hushed, impassioned murmur came from beyond. Miss Baker leaned forward shamelessly to listen. The murmur wavered on the edge of coherence, sank down, mounted excitedly, then ceased.

With my keen canine hearing, I could make out every word spoken in the other room. But being unable to speak, I was in no position to relay the private conversation to the humans at the table. I simply continued dozing by Nick's feet, keeping the overheard secrets to myself.

"This Mr. Gatsby you mentioned is my neighbor —" Nick said. I could tell he wanted a change in topic.

"Don't talk. I want to hear what happens."

"Is something happening?" he asked innocently.

"You mean you don't know?" said Miss Baker, genuinely surprised. "I thought everybody knew."

"I don't."

"Why—" she hesitated, "Tom's got some woman in New York."

"Got some woman?" Nick repeated blankly.

Miss Baker nodded. "She might have the decency not to call during dinner. Right?"

Before more could be said, Daisy and Tom returned in a flutter of fabric and a crunch of boots. I perked up my ears, catching the distinct scent of tension in the air. But the humans resumed dining as if nothing had occurred.

"It couldn't be helped!" Daisy cried with tense gaiety.

She sat down, glanced searchingly at Miss Baker, then at Nick, and continued: "I looked outside for a minute and it's very romantic out there. There's a bird on the lawn—I think it must be a nightingale that flew over on some ship. He's singing away—" her voice sang. "It's romantic, isn't it, Tom?"

"Very romantic," Tom replied miserably. Then to Nick: "If it's light enough after dinner, I want to show you the stables."

The telephone again rang inside, startlingly. As Daisy decisively shook her head at Tom— about the stables, about the phone call? It was unclear—all subjects vanished into air.

Among the fractured last minutes at the table, I remember the candles being relit pointlessly, and I sensed Nick wanted to look directly at everyone yet avoid all eyes. I couldn't guess Daisy and Tom's thoughts, but I doubt even Miss Baker, who seemed to have mastered a hardy skepticism, could fully ignore the shrill metallic urgency of that phone, that sixth, unseen guest. To some temperaments the situation might have seemed intriguing—my instinct in a situation like this would be to bark for help.

Needless to say, the horses went unmentioned again. Tom and Miss Baker strolled back to the library, as if standing vigil by a tangible body, while trying to appear pleasantly interested. With a little deafness, I followed Daisy and Nick onto the connecting porches to the front porch. In its deepening gloom, they sat together on a wicker settee. I settled contentedly on the porch near Nick's feet, resting my head on my paws.

Daisy held her face in her hands, feeling its shape, her eyes drifting into the velvet dusk. I sensed tumultuous emotions stir within her. Nick asked soothing questions about her daughter, I think meant to calm her.

"We don't know each other well, Nick, even as cousins. You didn't come to my wedding."

"I wasn't back from war," he replied.

"That's true." She hesitated. "Well, I've had a very bad time, Nick, and I'm pretty cynical about everything."

Evidently, she had reason to be. Nick waited, but Daisy said no more. After a moment he lamely returned to the subject of her daughter.

"I suppose she talks, and—eats, and everything."

"Oh, yes." Daisy looked at him absently. "Listen, Nick; let me tell you what I said when she was born. Would you like to hear?"

"Very much."

"It'll show you how I've gotten to feel about—things. Well, she was less than an hour old and Tom was God knows where. I woke up out of the ether with an utterly abandoned feeling and asked the nurse right away if it was a boy or a girl. She told me it was a girl, and so I turned my head away and wept. 'All right,' I said, 'I'm glad it's a girl. And I hope she'll be a fool—that's the best thing a girl can be in this world, a beautiful little fool.'

"You see, I think everything's terrible anyhow," she went on decisively. "Everybody thinks so—the most advanced people. And I know. I've been everywhere and seen everything and done everything."

Her eyes flashed defiantly, rather like Tom's, and she laughed with thrilling scorn. "Sophisticated—God, I'm sophisticated!"

The moment Daisy's voice trailed off, no longer gripping our attention and belief, I sensed an underlying falseness in her words. It troubled me, as though the entire evening had been a ruse somehow, to extract some emotional response from Nick. I waited, and as expected, Daisy soon glanced at him with an absolute smirk on her lovely face, as if declaring her membership in a rather elite secret society shared with Tom.

～

Inside, the crimson room glowed with light. Tom and Miss Baker sat at either end of the long couch as she read aloud from a magazine, her words flowing together soothingly. The lamplight shone on Tom's boots and glinted along the paper as Miss Baker turned a page, her slender arms fluttering.

When we entered, she silenced us a moment with a raised hand. "To be continued," she said, tossing the magazine down. "In our very next issue."

She stood restlessly, knee jiggling. "Ten o'clock," she remarked, eyeing the ceiling. "Time for this good girl to go to bed."

"Jordan's playing in a tournament tomorrow in Westchester," Daisy explained.

"Oh, you're Jordan Baker," Nick said. Like him, I now understood why she looked familiar: we'd seen her contemptuous expression in pictures of high society's sporting life. I also vaguely recalled hearing some humans offer an unpleasant story about her, long forgotten.

"Good night," Miss Baker said softly. "Wake me at eight, won't you?"

"If you'll get up."

"I will. Goodnight, Mr. Carraway. See you again."

"Of course, you will," Daisy confirmed. "In fact, I'll arrange a marriage. Come over often, Nick, and I'll fling you together—lock you in linen closets, push you out to sea, that sort of thing—"

"Good night," called Miss Baker, already on the stairs. "I haven't heard a word."

"She's a nice girl," said Tom after a moment. "They shouldn't let her gad about like this."

"Who shouldn't?" Daisy asked coldly.

"Her family."

"She's only got one ancient aunt. Besides, Nick will look after her, won't you? She'll spend lots of weekends here this summer. I think it'll be good for her."

Daisy and Tom exchanged a long, silent glance.

"Is she from New York?" Nick asked quickly.

"Louisville. We were girlhood friends there."

"Did you give Nick a little heart-to-heart on the veranda?" Tom interjected.

"Did I?" Daisy looked at Nick. "I can't recall, but I think we discussed Nordic races. Yes, I'm sure we did. It sort of crept up and the next thing you know—"

I was there and recall no mention of racing. Perhaps I had drifted off.

"Don't believe everything you hear, Nick," Tom advised.

Nick said lightly he'd heard nothing at all, and soon made motions to leave. They came to the door, standing side by side in the cheerful light. As we started the car, Daisy called out sharply, "Wait! I forgot to ask something important. We heard you were engaged to a girl out West."

"That's right," Tom affirmed. "We heard you were engaged."

"It's a lie. I'm too poor."

"But we heard it," Daisy insisted, opening up again vibrantly. "We heard it from three people, so it must be true."

Of course, I knew what Daisy and Tom referred to, but Nick wasn't even vaguely engaged. Rumors had spread the false news, which was partly why we'd come East. You can't stop being friends over gossip, yet I knew he had no plans to be rumored into marriage.

Their interest rather touched me and made them less remotely rich—nevertheless, as we drove away, I felt confused and a little disgusted. It seemed to me that the thing for Daisy to do was to rush out of the house, child in arms—but apparently there were no such intentions in her head. As for Tom, the fact that he "had some woman in New York" was really less surprising than that he had been depressed by a book. Something was making him nibble at the edge of stale ideas, as if his sturdy physical egotism no longer nourished his peremptory heart.

Already it was deep summer on roadhouse roofs and in front of wayside garages, where new red gas-pumps sat out in pools of light. When we reached the estate at West Egg, Nick ran the motorcar under its shed, and we sat for a while on an abandoned grass roller in the yard.

The wind had blown off, leaving a loud bright night with wings beating in the trees and a persistent organ sound, as the full bellows of the earth blew the frogs full of life. The silhouette of a moving cat wavered across the moonlight and turning my head to watch it, I saw that we were not alone—fifty feet away a figure had emerged from the shadow of my neighbor's mansion and was standing with his hands in his pockets regarding the silver pepper of the stars.

Something in his leisurely movements and the secure position of his feet upon the lawn suggested that it was Mr. Gatsby himself, come out to determine what share was his of our local heavens.

Nick seemed ready to call to him. Miss Baker had mentioned him at dinner, and that would do for an introduction. But the man gave a sudden intimation that he was content to be alone—he stretched out his arms toward the dark water in a curious way, and far as I was from him, I could have sworn he was trembling. Involuntarily Nick and I glanced seaward—and we distinguished nothing except a single green light, minute and far away, that might have been the end of a dock.

When we looked once more for Gatsby he had vanished, and we were alone again in the unquiet darkness.

Chapter Two

About halfway between West Egg and New York, the road hastily joins the railroad and runs beside it a quarter mile, shrinking from a desolate valley of ashes—a strange farm where ashes grow in ridges like wheat, forming grotesque gardens and ghostly houses, chimneys and rising smoke. Dim figures move crumbling through the powdery air, already disintegrating. Occasionally, a line of gray cars crawls down an invisible track, screeching to a rest. Ash-gray men swarm up with leaden spades, stirring an impenetrable cloud that hides their obscure work.

But above the gray land and bleak drifting dust, you eventually perceive the eyes of Doctor T.J. Eckleburg— blue and gigantic, the retinas a yard high. They gaze out from enormous yellow spectacles over a nonexistent nose. Some oculist with a morbid sense of humor clearly put the billboards there to attract patients in Queens before sinking into eternal blindness himself or leaving town. The eyes brood dimly over the dumping ground, weathered by sun and rain.

The valley borders a small foul river. When the drawbridge rises for barges, waiting train passengers can stare at the dismal scene for half an hour. It was here I first encountered Tom's mistress, thanks to a mandatory halt.

Though curious, I had no desire to meet her—but Nick did. One afternoon we traveled to New York and when we stopped at the ash heaps, Tom sprang up and dragged my master from the train car. I followed at a slower, less interested pace.

"We're getting off!" Tom insisted, seemingly fortified from lunch. His determination to have Nick's company bordered on violence. He arrogantly assumed that on a Sunday afternoon we had nothing better to do.

The two of us followed him, walking back a hundred yards under Doctor Eckleburg's constant stare. The only visible building was a small yellow block sitting on the wasteland's edge, a makeshift Main Street ministering to nothing beyond. One of its three shops was for rent, another an all-night diner with an ashen, unappealing path and an odor which held me at bay. The third was a garage: *Repairs. GEORGE B. WILSON. Cars Bought and Sold.*

I accompanied the two men inside.

The interior was bare and unprosperous; the only visible car was a dust-cloaked wreck of a Ford crouching dimly in a corner. I'd imagined sumptuous apartments concealed above this shadowy garage, but the wan, faintly handsome proprietor appeared, wiping his hands on waste. His pale blue eyes gleamed damply with desperate hope at the sight of us.

"Hello Wilson, old man," Tom said jovially, clapping his shoulder. "How's business?"

"Can't complain," Wilson replied unconvincingly. "When will you sell me that car?"

"Next week. My man's working on it now."

"Works pretty slow, don't he?"

"No, he doesn't," Tom retorted coldly. "Maybe I should sell it elsewhere if you feel that way."

"I didn't mean that," Wilson explained quickly. "I just meant—"

Wilson's voice faded as Tom glanced impatiently around. Then footsteps descended and a woman's plump figure blocked the office light. She was in her mid-thirties, carrying extra weight sensuously.

Her spotted dark blue dress contained no trace of beauty, yet she had an immediately perceptible vitality, as if her nerves smoldered constantly. She smiled slowly, passing through Wilson as if he were a ghost, and shook Tom's hand while staring him in the eye. Then without turning, she spoke softly and coarsely to her husband:

"Get some chairs so someone can sit."

"Oh, sure," Wilson agreed hurriedly, blending into the cement-colored walls as he went to the office. Pale dust veiled his dark suit and hair, as it veiled everything except his wife, who moved closer to Tom.

"I want to see you," Tom said intensely. "Get on the next train."

"All right."

"I'll meet you at the newsstand downstairs at the station."

She nodded and moved away just as Wilson emerged with two chairs.

We waited down the road, out of sight. It was a few days before the Fourth of July—a scrawny Italian child lined up torpedoes along the tracks.

"Terrible place, isn't it," said Tom, exchanging a frown with Doctor Eckleburg's eyes.

"Awful."

"It's good for her to get away."

"Doesn't her husband object?" Nick asked.

"Wilson? He thinks she visits her sister. He's so dumb, he doesn't know he's alive."

So, Tom, his girl, Nick and myself rode up together to New York—though not precisely together, since Mrs. Wilson discreetly sat apart. Tom deferred that much to the propriety of any East Eggers on board.

At the station, she bought a tabloid and movie magazine. In the drugstore, cold cream and perfume. She changed into a tight brown dress and then Tom helped her onto the platform. Upstairs, she dismissed four taxis before selecting a lavender one with gray upholstery. We slid from the bustling station into sunshine. Abruptly she tapped the front glass.

"I want one of those dogs," she said earnestly. "For the apartment. They're nice to have—a dog. Not a big dog, like that one," she added, gesturing dismissively in my direction. "Something I can hold in my hands."

We backed toward an old man resembling John D. Rockefeller. A dozen puppies of indistinct breed cowered in his basket.

"What kind are they?" Mrs. Wilson asked eagerly as he approached.

"All kinds. What kind you want, lady?"

"A police dog would be nice. You don't have those, do you?"

The man dubiously plunged his hand into the basket and extracted a wriggling pup by the scruff, which yelped faintly. My hackles rose in concern.

"That's no police dog," said Tom drily. I silently agreed with his assessment.

"No, not exactly police..." the man replied, disappointed. "More of an Airedale." He rubbed the pup's ragged brown fur. "Some coat, eh? Won't ever catch cold."

"I think he's cute!" Mrs. Wilson cooed. "How much?"

"Ten dollars for that one."

The pup—undoubtedly part Airedale despite his white feet—settled onto Mrs. Wilson's lap as she stroked his coat lovingly. The other pups whimpered, stirring my caretaking instincts.

"Boy or girl?" she asked.

"Boy."

"It's a bitch," Tom snapped. "Here's cash. Buy ten more with it."

I studied the cavalier wealthy pair. If only I could

give those puppies a proper home. But as a mere dog, I could only observe this human folly once again.

~

We drove to Fifth Avenue, so warm and pastoral that Sunday afternoon, I half-expected to see a great flock of white sheep around the corner. It would have been a refreshing sight.

"Hold on, I should leave you here," Nick said.

"No, you don't," Tom interjected quickly. "Myrtle will be hurt if you don't come up." Turning to her, "Won't you, Myrtle?"

"Come on," she urged. "I'll call my sister Catherine. People say she's a beauty."

I could smell my master's hesitation, but his polite nature kept him from refusing outright.

We continued over the Park towards the West Hundreds. At 158th, the cab stopped before a long white apartment building. With a regal glance around, Mrs. Wilson gathered her things—and the young, squirming pup—and haughtily entered.

"I'll have the McKees come over," she announced in the elevator, her shrill perfume overpowering in the confined space. "And my sister, of course."

The top floor apartment was filled with a clutter of fancy human furniture, the abundance of scents and obstacles disorienting my dog senses like getting lost in a massive kennel full of unfamiliar smells. The only picture was a large photograph of a hen that from afar looked like an old lady's face beaming down. Tabloids and scandal sheets lay scattered about, along with a Bible.

Mrs. Wilson first saw to her new puppy. A reluctant elevator boy fetched straw and biscuits—one which slowly disintegrated in the saucer as the afternoon passed. It didn't even look appetizing to me, and I hadn't eaten in several hours. Meanwhile Tom retrieved whiskey from a cabinet.

I had only seen Nick drunk twice before in life—this would be the latter instance. So, I imagine the day has a dim, hazy quality in his memory, though sunlight filled the rooms until after eight.

Sitting in Tom's lap, Mrs. Wilson chattered on the phone. With no cigarettes, Nick and I were sent to the store. When we returned, the couple had vanished, so Nick discreetly read a book and I just as discreetly napped.

The moment Tom and Myrtle reappeared, more company began arriving. I lifted my nose, alert to these strange newcomers.

The sister Catherine was a slender, worldly woman with bobbed red hair and powder-white complexion. Her redrawn eyebrows looked blurred as nature tried realigning them. Countless bracelets jangled loudly with her every move. She entered possessively, surveying the furniture as if it were her own. When asked, she laughed shrilly, repeated the question aloud, and said she lived with a girlfriend.

Mr. McKee was a pale, feminine man from downstairs, a spot of shaving lather still on his cheekbone. He politely greeted everyone, and I gathered he was the photographer behind the hazy enlarged photo of Mrs. Wilson's mother on the wall. His wife was handsome yet dreadful—she proudly announced he'd photographed her 127 times since marriage.

Mrs. Wilson had changed her costume again and was now attired in an elaborate afternoon dress of cream-colored chiffon, which gave out a continual rustle as she swept about the room. With the influence of the dress, her personality had also undergone a change. The intense vitality that had been so remarkable in the garage was converted into impressive hauteur. Her laughter, her gestures, her assertions became more violently affected moment by moment, and as she expanded the room grew smaller around her, until she seemed to be revolving on a noisy, creaking pivot through the smoky air.

"My dear," she told her sister in a high mincing shout, "most of these fellas will cheat you every time. All they think of is money. I had a woman up here last week to look at my feet and when she gave me the bill, you'd of thought she had my appendicitus out."

"What was the name of the woman?" asked Mrs. McKee.

"Mrs. Eberhardt. She goes around looking at people's feet in their own homes."

"I like your dress," remarked Mrs. McKee, "I think it's adorable."

Mrs. Wilson rejected the compliment by raising her eyebrow in disdain. "It's just a crazy old thing," she said. "I just slip it on sometimes when I don't care what I look like."

"But it looks wonderful on you, if you know what I mean," pursued Mrs. McKee. "If Chester could only get you in that pose, I think he could make something of it."

We all looked silently at Mrs. Wilson, who removed a hair strand from her eyes and smiled brilliantly back at us. Mr. McKee studied her intently with tilted head, then slowly waved his hand before his face.

"I should change the light," he said after a moment. "I'd like to bring out the modeling of the features. And I'd try to get hold of all the back hair."

"I wouldn't change the light!" cried Mrs. McKee. "I think it's—"

Her husband shushed her, and we gazed at the subject again until Tom Buchanan audibly yawned and stood up.

"Have a drink, McKees," he said. "More ice and mineral water, Myrtle, before we all sleep."

She looked down at me, in my spot on the floor, and laughed for no reason. Then she swooped over to her puppy, kissed it ecstatically, and flounced into the kitchen, as if a dozen chefs awaited orders.

"I've done nice work out on Long Island," boasted Mr. McKee.

Tom stared blankly until McKee clarified, "Two studies: 'Montauk Point—the Gulls' and 'Montauk Point—the Sea'."

The sister Catherine sat beside Nick on the couch, stepping gingerly over me in the process. "Do you live on Long Island too?" she asked.

"We're in West Egg," Nick replied, with a nod toward me.

"Oh really? I was at a party there, thrown by a man named Gatsby. Do you know him?"

"I'm his next-door neighbor."

"Well, they say he's Kaiser Wilhelm's nephew— that's his money source."

"Is that so?"

She nodded. "He scares me. I'd hate to cross him."

Mrs. McKee suddenly pointed at Catherine, interrupting the gossip about our neighbor. "Chester, I think you could do something with her!" But Mr. McKee only nodded in a bored way before turning back to Tom.

"I'd like more work on Long Island if I could get access. Just give me a start."

"Ask Myrtle," said Tom, laughing as Mrs. Wilson entered with a tray. "She'll give you an intro to her husband so you can paint him—'George B. Wilson at the Gas Pump' or something."

Catherine whispered to Nick. "Neither can stand their spouse."

"Can't they?"

"Can't stand them." She looked between Myrtle and Tom. "Why stay married then? I'd divorce and remarry immediately."

"Doesn't she like Wilson either?"

Myrtle overheard and responded with violent, obscene words.

"You see?" said Catherine triumphantly, lowering

her voice again. "It's his wife keeping them apart. She won't allow divorce."

I was confused, having no grasp of human matrimony customs.

"When they do marry, they'll go out west until it blows over," Catherine continued.

"Europe would be more discreet."

"Oh, you like Europe?" she exclaimed, surprised. "I just got back from Monte Carlo."

"Really?"

"Last year with a girlfriend. We went to Monte Carlo and back through Marseilles. We had over twelve hundred dollars but lost it all gambling in two days. It was awful getting back, I can tell you. God, how I hated that town!"

The late sky momentarily bloomed an azure Mediterranean hue in the window before Mrs. McKee's shrill voice pierced my ears, calling us back inside.

"I nearly made a mistake too," she declared loudly. My sensitive hearing cringed at her vigorous tone. "I almost married a little jerk who'd chased me for years. Everyone kept saying 'Lucille, he's way below you!' But if not for Chester, he'd have gotten me for sure."

"Yes, but you didn't marry him," Myrtle nodded, the bracelets on her arms jangling with the motion. The noise grated on my canine senses.

"I know I didn't."

"Well, I did," said Myrtle, her words tinged with an ambiguity beyond my understanding. "That's the difference with your case and mine."

"Why did you, Myrtle?" Catherine demanded. Her authoritative stance reminded me of an alpha dog correcting a lower pack member.

Myrtle considered, twirling her gaudy bracelets nervously. "I thought he was a gentleman. That he knew breeding. But he wasn't fit to lick my shoe."

"You were crazy for him awhile," said Catherine, examining her nails.

"Crazy for him!" Myrtle cried incredulously, the pitch piercing my sensitive ears and making them pin back. "I was never any crazier for him than that man there!"

She pointed suddenly at Nick, and everyone looked at him accusingly. He tried to indicate through cautious body language that he'd played no part in her past. I moved closer to him, prepared to defend if needed.

"The only *crazy* I was was when I married him. I knew right away I made a mistake. He borrowed somebody's best suit to get married in and never even told me about it, and the man came after it one day when he was out."

She looked around to see who was listening. "'Oh, is that your suit?' I said. 'This is the first I ever heard about it.' But I gave it to him and then I lay down and cried to beat the band all afternoon."

"She really ought to get away from him," resumed Catherine to Nick. "They've been living over that garage for eleven years. And Tom's the first sweetie she ever had."

The bottle of whiskey—a second one—was now in

constant demand by all present, excepting Catherine who "felt just as good on nothing at all." Tom rang for the janitor and sent him for some celebrated sandwiches, which were a complete supper in themselves. Nick slipped me several morsels under the table. Though the human chatter remained a mystery, I was content at his side, enjoying his generous treat.

I wanted to get out and walk eastward toward the park through the soft twilight with Nick, but each time we tried to go, he became entangled in some wild strident argument which pulled him back, as if with ropes, into his chair.

Myrtle pulled her chair close to Nick, and suddenly her warm breath poured over him the story of her first meeting with Tom.

"It was on the two little seats facing each other that are always the last ones left on the train. I was going up to New York to see my sister and spend the night. He had on a dress suit and patent leather shoes, and I couldn't keep my eyes off him, but every time he looked at me, I had to pretend to be looking at the advertisement over his head. When we came into the station, he was next to me and his white shirt-front pressed against my arm—and so I told him I'd have to call a policeman, but he knew I lied. I was so excited that when I got into a taxi with him, I didn't hardly know I wasn't getting into a subway train. All I kept thinking about, over and over, was 'You can't live forever, you can't live forever.'"

She turned to Mrs. McKee and the room rang full of her artificial laughter.

"My dear," she cried, "I'm going to give you this dress as soon as I'm through with it. I've got to get another one tomorrow. I'm going to make a list of all the things I've got to get. A massage and a wave and a collar for the dog and one of those cute little ashtrays where you touch a spring, and a wreath with a black silk bow for mother's grave that'll last all summer. I got to write down a list, so I won't forget all the things I got to do."

It was nine o'clock—almost immediately afterward I saw Nick check his watch and found it was ten. Mr. McKee was asleep on a chair with his fists clenched in his lap, like a photograph of a man of action. As Nick took out his handkerchief, I sniffed curiously at the spot of dried lather on McKee's cheek that had bothered me all afternoon. Nick gently wiped it away.

The little puppy was sitting on the table, looking with blind eyes through the smoke and from time to time groaning faintly. The humans around me disappeared, reappeared, made plans to go somewhere, and then lost each other, searching and finding one another just feet away.

Some time toward midnight, Tom Buchanan and Mrs. Wilson stood face to face, discussing in impassioned voices whether Mrs. Wilson had any right to mention Daisy's name.

"Daisy! Daisy! Daisy!" shouted Mrs. Wilson. "I'll say it whenever I want to! Daisy! Dai—"

With a short, deft movement, Tom Buchanan broke her nose with his open hand.

Then there were bloody towels upon the bathroom

floor, and women's voices scolding, and high over the confusion a long, broken wail of pain. Mr. McKee awoke from his doze and started in a daze toward the door. When he had gone halfway, he turned around and stared at the scene—his wife and Catherine stumbling among the crowded furniture with articles of aid, and the despairing figure on the couch bleeding fluently.

Mr. McKee then turned and continued out the door. Nick took his hat from the chandelier, and I followed him closely, eager to leave the chaotic and bewildering scene.

"Come to lunch someday," McKee suggested, as we all groaned descending in the elevator.

"Where?" Nick replied.

"Anywhere."

"Keep your hands off the lever," the elevator boy snapped.

"I beg your pardon," McKee said with dignity, "I didn't know I was touching it."

"All right," Nick agreed. "I'll be glad to."

After the chaotic night, Nick and I helped escort the dazed and stumbling Mr. McKee to his bed. I watched curiously as Nick eased McKee into the sheets. Still clad only in his underwear, McKee fumbled through a large portfolio clutched in his hands.

"Beauty and the Beast...Loneliness...Old Grocery Horse...Brook'n Bridge..." he mumbled, gazing at photos from his work.

Soon after, I lay half asleep on the cold floor of the

Pennsylvania Station, Nick staring at a newspaper as we awaited the four o'clock train. Exhausted from the chaotic night, I dozed contently by my loyal master's feet, the familiar smell of his shoes a comfort amidst the bustling station commotion.

Chapter Three

There was music drifting from Gatsby's mansion through the summer nights. In his gardens, men and women fluttered about like squirrels amongst whispers, champagne, and stars. At high tide in the afternoon, I watched his guests diving off his raft or sunning themselves on the hot sand, while motorboats cut across the Sound, pulling humans on strange floating boards over foaming wakes.

On weekends, his Rolls-Royce turned into a bus, ferrying revelers to and from the city between breakfast time and past midnight, while his station wagon scurried around like a yellow beetle to meet all trains. And on Mondays, eight servants including an extra gardener toiled all day with mops and brushes and hammers and shears, repairing the damage from the wild nights before.

Every Friday, five crates of oranges and lemons

arrived from a New York fruit vendor—and every Monday these same fruits left Gatsby's back door as mounds of dried pulp. There was a machine in the kitchen that could squeeze the juice from two hundred oranges in half an hour—if you possessed nimble fingers and pressed the button two hundred times.

At least once a fortnight, caterers arrived with tents and colored lights to transform Gatsby's gardens into a Christmas tree. His buffet tables were piled high with gleaming treats and glazed hams that made my mouth water, vivid salads, pastries shaped like animals, and bronzed turkeys. In the main hall, a bar with a real brass rail was set up, and stocked with gins and liquors and with cordials so long forgotten that most of his female guests were too young to know one from another.

By seven o'clock, the whole orchestra had arrived —not just a small group, but a whole pack of instruments filling the pit with music. The last swimmers had come in from the beach now and were dressing upstairs; the cars from New York were parked five deep in the drive, and already the halls and salons and verandas were gaudy with primary colors and hair shorn in strange new ways and shawls beyond the dreams of Castile. The bar was in full swing and floating rounds of cocktails permeated the garden outside until the air was alive with chatter and laughter and casual innuendo and introductions forgotten on the spot and enthusiastic meetings between women who never knew each other's names.

The lights grew brighter as the earth lurched away

from the sun and then the orchestra was playing yellow cocktail music and the opera of voices pitched a key higher. The party had begun.

I believe that on the first night Nick and I went to Gatsby's house, we were some of the few guests who had actually been invited. People were not invited—they just went there, cramming into cars that bore them out to Long Island where they ended up at Gatsby's door. Once there, they were introduced by somebody who knew Gatsby and after that they conducted themselves according to the rules of behavior associated with amusement parks. Sometimes they came and went without having met Gatsby at all, arriving with a simplicity of heart that was its own ticket of admission.

Nick and I had been formally invited. A chauffeur in a uniform of robin's egg blue crossed our lawn early that Saturday morning with a surprisingly formal note from his employer—the honor would be entirely Gatsby's, it said, if Nick and his charming greyhound would attend his "little party" that night. Gatsby had seen us around and had intended to call on us long before, but a peculiar combination of circumstances had prevented it—the note was signed Jay Gatsby in a majestic hand.

Nick (dressed up in white flannels) and I went over a little after seven and wandered around rather ill-at-ease among swirls and eddies of people neither of us knew—though here and there was a face I had noticed on the commuting train. I was immediately struck by the number of young Englishmen dotted about; all well dressed, all looking a little hungry and all talking in low earnest voices to solid and prosperous Americans. I was sure that they were selling something: bonds or insurance or automobiles. They were, at least, agonizingly aware of the easy money in the vicinity and convinced that it was theirs for a few words in the right key.

As soon as we arrived, we made an attempt to find our host, but the two or three people of whom Nick asked Gatsby's whereabouts stared at us in such an amazed way and denied so vehemently any knowledge of his movements that we slunk off in the direction of the cocktail table—the only place in the garden where a man and his dog could linger without looking purposeless and alone.

Nick was on his way to getting roaring drunk from sheer embarrassment when Jordan Baker came out of the house and stood at the head of the marble steps, leaning a little backward and looking with contemptuous interest down into the garden.

Although I was at peace with just his company, Nick found it necessary to attach himself to someone before we could begin addressing the other partygoers cordially.

"Hello!" Nick roared, as we approached Jordan Baker. His voice seemed unnaturally loud across the garden.

"I thought you might be here," Jordan responded absently as we came up. "I remembered you lived next door to—"

She took Nick's hand impersonally, promising to take care of us in a minute, as she turned her attention to two girls in matching yellow dresses who had stopped at the bottom of the steps.

"Hello!" the pair cried together. "Sorry you didn't win."

I surmised that was about Jordan's recent loss in the golf finals.

"You don't know who we are," said one of the yellow-clad girls. "But we met you here about a month ago."

"You've dyed your hair since then," remarked Jordan, but the girls had moved casually on and her remark was addressed to the premature moon, produced like the supper, no doubt, out of a caterer's basket.

With Jordan's slender golden arm resting in Nick's, we descended the steps and sauntered about the garden. A tray of cocktails floated at us through the twilight, and we sat down at a table with the two girls in yellow, and three men, each one introduced to us as Mr. Mumble.

"Do you come to these parties often?" Jordan inquired of the girl beside her.

"The last one was the one I met you at," the girl answered confidently, before turning to her friend. "Wasn't it, Lucille?"

It was for Lucille, too.

"I like to come," Lucille said. "I never care what I do, so I always have a good time. When I was here last, I tore my gown on a chair, and Gatsby asked my name and address—inside of a week I got a package from Croirier's with a new evening gown in it."

"Did you keep it?" asked Jordan.

"Sure I did. I was going to wear it tonight, but it was too big in the bust and had to be altered. It was gas blue with lavender beads. Two hundred and sixty-five dollars."

"There's something funny about a fellow that'll do a thing like that," said the other girl eagerly. "He doesn't want any trouble with anybody."

"Who doesn't?" Nick inquired.

"Gatsby. Somebody told me—"

The two girls and Jordan leaned together confidentially. From my spot under the table, my ears perked up.

"Somebody told me they thought he killed a man once."

A thrill passed over all of us. The three Mr. Mumbles bent forward and listened eagerly.

"I don't think it's so much that," argued Lucille skeptically. "It's more that he was a German spy during the war."

One of the men nodded in confirmation.

"I heard that from a man who knew all about him, grew up with him in Germany," he assured us positively.

"Oh, no," said the first girl. "It couldn't be *that*, because he was in the American army during the war." As our credulity switched back to her, she leaned forward with excitement. "You look at him sometimes when he thinks nobody's looking at him. I'll bet he killed a man."

She narrowed her eyes and shivered. Lucille shivered too. We all turned and searched for Gatsby in the crowded garden. It was a testament to the romantic speculation Gatsby inspired that there were whispers about him from those who found little that it was necessary to whisper about in this world.

The first supper—there would be another after midnight—was now being served. Jordan invited Nick and I to join her group, spread around a table across the garden. There were three married couples and Jordan's escort, a persistent undergraduate given to violent innuendo and obviously under the impression that sooner or later Jordan was going to yield him up her person to a greater or lesser degree. Unlike the rambunctious partygoers, this group maintained a dignified air, representing the genteel nobility of the countryside—East Egg condescending to West Egg's showy revelry.

"Let's get out," Jordan whispered after a wasted half hour of polite chatter. "This is too polite for me."

We got up, and Jordan explained we were going to find our elusive host, whom we had yet to meet. The undergraduate nodded in a cynical, melancholy way.

The bar, where we glanced first, was crowded, but Gatsby was not there. She couldn't find him from the top of the steps, and he wasn't on the veranda. On a chance, we tried an important-looking door, and walked into a high Gothic library, paneled with carved

English oak, and probably transported complete from some ruin overseas.

A stout, middle-aged man with enormous owl-eyed spectacles was sitting somewhat drunk on the edge of a great table, staring with unsteady concentration at the shelves of books. As we entered, he wheeled excitedly around and examined Jordan from head to foot.

"What do you think?" he demanded impetuously.

"About what?" Nick asked.

The man waved his hand toward the bookshelves. "About that. No need to bother ascertaining. I already ascertained. They're real."

Nick was puzzled. "The books?"

The man nodded eagerly. "Absolutely real—pages and everything! I thought they'd be fake cardboard props. But matter of fact, they're genuine books. Pages and—Here! Lemme show you."

Taking our skepticism for granted, he rushed to the bookcases and returned with Volume One of *The Stoddard Lectures*.

"See!" he cried triumphantly. "It's a bona fide piece of printed matter. It fooled me. This fella's a regular Belasco. It's a triumph. What thoroughness! What realism! Knew when to stop too—didn't cut the pages. But what do you want? What do you expect?"

The man snatched the book back, hastily replacing it and muttering that removing one brick could make the whole library collapse.

"Who brought you here?" he demanded of us suddenly. "Or did you just come? I was brought. Most people were brought."

Jordan looked at him alertly, cheerfully, without answering.

"I was brought by a woman named Roosevelt," he continued. "Mrs. Claud Roosevelt. Do you know her? I met her somewhere last night. I've been drunk for about a week now, and I thought it might sober me up to sit in a library."

Nick played along. "Has it worked?"

"A little bit, I think. Hard to tell yet. I've only been here an hour. Did I mention the books are real? They're—"

"You told us," Nick interjected politely.

Nick shook hands with him gravely, I gave him a cheerful nod, and we went back outdoors.

There was dancing now on the canvas in the garden, old men pushing young girls backward in eternal graceless circles, superior couples holding each other tortuously, fashionably and keeping in the corners— and a great number of single girls dancing individualistically or relieving the orchestra for a moment of the burden of the banjo or the traps.

By midnight the hilarity had increased. A celebrated tenor had sung in Italian and a notorious contralto had sung in jazz and between the numbers people were doing "stunts" all over the garden, while happy vacuous bursts of laughter rose toward the summer sky.

A pair of stage "twins"—who turned out to be the

girls in yellow—did a baby act in costume, and champagne was served in glasses bigger than finger bowls. The moon had risen higher, and floating in the Sound was a triangle of silver scales, trembling a little to the stiff, tinny drip of the banjoes on the lawn.

Nick and I were still with Jordan Baker. We were sitting at a table with a man of about Nick's age and a rowdy little girl who gave way upon the slightest provocation to uncontrollable laughter. Nick seemed to be enjoying himself now. He had taken two finger bowls of champagne and I think the scene had changed before his eyes into something significant, elemental and profound.

At a lull in the entertainment, the man looked at Nick and smiled.

"Your face is familiar," he said, politely. "Weren't you in the Third Division during the war?"

"Why, yes. I was in the Ninth Machine-Gun Battalion."

"I was in the Seventh Infantry until June nineteen-eighteen. I knew I'd seen you somewhere before."

They talked for a moment about some wet, grey little villages in France. Evidently, he lived in this vicinity, for he told Nick that he had just bought a hydroplane and was going to try it out in the morning.

"Want to go with me, old sport? Just near the shore along the Sound."

"What time?"

"Any time that suits you best."

It was on the tip of Nick's tongue to ask his name when Jordan looked around and smiled.

"Having a gay time now?" she inquired.

"Much better." Nick turned again to the man. "This is an unusual party for me. I haven't even seen the host. We—" he gestured toward me, in my spot on the grass, and then waved his hand at the invisible hedge in the distance. "We live over there. And this man Gatsby sent over his chauffeur with an invitation."

For a moment the man looked at Nick as if he failed to understand.

"I'm Gatsby," the man said suddenly.

"What!" Nick exclaimed in surprise. "Oh, I beg your pardon."

I had recognized him, of course, as the man we'd seen on that earlier night, Staring at the green light across the bay. I assumed Nick recognized Gatsby as well, but of course his sight was less acute than mine.

"I thought you knew, old sport. I'm afraid I'm not a very good host."

Gatsby smiled warmly, reassuringly—one of those rare smiles containing eternal reassurance. For an instant, it seemed to face the whole external world, before concentrating on Nick with irresistible favor. It understood him just as far as Nick wished to be understood, believed in Nick as Nick wanted to believe in himself, and conveyed precisely the impression Nick hoped to at his best.

Precisely at that point it vanished—and I was looking at an elegant young rough-neck, a year or two over thirty, whose elaborate formality of speech just missed being absurd. Several times, before he introduced himself, I'd got a strong impression that he was picking his words with care.

Almost at the moment when Mr. Gatsby identified himself, a butler hurried toward him with the information that Chicago was calling him on the wire. Gatsby excused himself with a small bow that included each of us in turn. I was pleased he went so far as to acknowledge not only his guests, but the dogs of his guests as well.

"If you want anything, just ask, old sport," he urged Nick. "Excuse me. I'll rejoin you shortly."

After he left, Nick turned to Jordan, seeming startled. I sensed Nick had pictured Mr. Gatsby as an older, heavier figure.

"Who is he?" Nick asked incredulously. "Do you know?"

"He's just a man named Gatsby."

"Where is he from, I mean? And what does he do?"

"Now you're started on the subject," she answered with a wan smile. "Well—he told me once he was an Oxford man." A dim background started to take shape behind him, but at her next remark it faded away. "However, I don't believe it."

"Why not?"

"I don't know," she insisted. "I just don't think he went there."

Something in her tone reminded me of the other girl's remark, "I think he killed a man," and had the effect of stimulating our curiosity. I think Nick would have accepted without question the information that Gatsby sprang from the swamps of Louisiana or from the lower East Side of New York. That was comprehensible. But young men didn't—at least in our provincial inexperience, we believed they didn't—drift coolly out of nowhere and buy a palace on Long Island Sound.

"Anyhow, he gives large parties," said Jordan, changing the subject with an urbane distaste for the concrete. "And I like large parties. They're so intimate. At small parties, there isn't any privacy."

There was the boom of a bass drum, and the voice of the orchestra leader rang out suddenly above the echolalia of the garden.

"Ladies and gentlemen," he cried. "At the request of Mr. Gatsby, we are going to play for you Mr. Vladimir Tostoff's latest work, which attracted so much attention at Carnegie Hall last May. If you read the papers, you know there was a big sensation." He smiled with jovial condescension and added "Some sensation!" whereupon everybody laughed.

"The piece is known," he concluded lustily, "as 'Vladimir Tostoff's Jazz History of the World.'"

The nature of Mr. Tostoff's composition eluded me, because just as it began, my eyes fell on Gatsby, standing alone on the marble steps and looking from one group to another with approving eyes. His tanned skin was drawn attractively tight on his face and his short hair looked as though it were trimmed every day. I could see nor sense anything sinister about him. I wondered if the fact that he was not drinking helped to set him off from his guests, for it seemed to me that he grew more correct as the fraternal hilarity increased.

I may have been mistaken, but Gatsby, Nick and I might have been the only sober figures in attendance, with the exception of the servants and a large percentage of the band.

When the "Jazz History of the World" was over, girls were putting their heads on men's shoulders in a puppyish, convivial way, girls were swooning backward playfully into men's arms, even into groups knowing that someone would arrest their falls—but no one swooned backward on Gatsby and no French bob touched Gatsby's shoulder and no singing quartets were formed with Gatsby's head for one link.

"I beg your pardon."

Gatsby's butler was suddenly standing beside us.

The butler turned to Jordan. "Miss Baker? I beg your pardon, but Mr. Gatsby would like to speak to you alone."

"With me?" Jordan exclaimed in surprise.

"Yes, madame."

She rose slowly, raising her eyebrows at Nick in puzzlement as she followed the butler toward the house. I noticed Jordan's movements had a jaunty athleticism, as if she'd learned to walk on crisp golf course mornings. It was a walk similar to that of a greyhound, on race day, proudly headed toward the paddock.

With Jordan gone, I was alone as Nick checked his watch and saw it was almost two o'clock. For some time, confused and intriguing sounds had floated from the long, many-windowed room overhanging the terrace. Dodging Jordan's drunk undergraduate—now engaged in lewd conversation with chorus girls—Nick and I went inside, impelled by the interesting sounds.

The large room was full of people. One of the girls in yellow was playing the piano and beside her stood a tall, red haired young lady from a famous chorus, engaged in song. She had drunk a quantity of champagne and during the course of her song she had decided ineptly that everything was very, very sad—she was not only singing, but she was also weeping.

Whenever there was a pause in the song, she filled it with gasping broken sobs, and then took up the lyric again in a quavering soprano. The tears coursed down her cheeks—not freely, however, for when they came into contact with her heavily beaded eyelashes, they assumed an inky color, and pursued the rest of their way in slow black rivulets.

A humorous suggestion was made that she sing the notes on her face, whereupon she threw up her hands, sank into a chair and went off into a deep vinous sleep.

"She had a fight with a man who says he's her husband," a girl beside us explained.

I looked around. Most of the remaining women were now having fights with men said to be their husbands. Even Jordan's party, the quartet from East Egg, were rent asunder by dissension.

One of the men was talking with curious intensity to a young actress, and his wife, after attempting to laugh at the situation in a dignified and indifferent way, broke down entirely and resorted to flank attacks—at intervals she appeared suddenly at his side like an angry diamond, and hissed "You promised!" into his ear.

~

The reluctance to go home was not confined to wayward men. The hall was at present occupied by two deplorably sober men and their highly indignant wives. The wives were sympathizing with each other in slightly raised voices.

"Whenever he sees I'm having a good time he wants to go home."

"Never heard anything so selfish in my life."

"We're always the first ones to leave."

"So are we."

"Well, we're almost the last tonight," said one of the men sheepishly. "The orchestra left half an hour ago."

In spite of the wives' agreement that such malevolence was beyond credibility, the dispute ended in a short struggle, and both wives were lifted kicking into the night.

As Nick and I waited for his hat in the hall, the door of the library opened, and Jordan Baker and Gatsby came out together. He was saying some last word to her, but the eagerness in his manner tightened abruptly into formality as several people approached him to say goodbye.

Jordan's party were calling impatiently to her from the porch, but she lingered for a moment to shake hands.

"I've just heard the most amazing thing," she whispered. "How long were we in there?"

"Why—about an hour."

"It was—simply amazing," she repeated abstractedly. "But I swore I wouldn't tell it and here I am tantalizing you." She yawned gracefully in Nick's face. "Please come and see me...Phone book...Under the name of Mrs. Sigourney Howard...My aunt..."

She was hurrying off as she talked—her brown hand waved a jaunty salute as she melted into her party at the door.

Rather ashamed that on our first appearance we had stayed so late, we joined the last of Gatsby's guests who were clustered around him. Nick explained that we'd hunted for him early in the evening and apologized for not having known him in the garden.

"Don't mention it," he enjoined Nick eagerly. "Don't give it another thought, old sport." The familiar expression held no more familiarity than the hand which reassuringly brushed Nick's shoulder and which gave my own back a friendly pat. "And don't forget we're going up in the hydroplane tomorrow morning at nine o'clock."

Then the butler, behind his shoulder: "Philadelphia wants you on the phone, sir."

"All right, in a minute. Tell them I'll be right there...good night."

"Good night."

"Good night." He smiled—and suddenly there seemed to be a pleasant significance in having been among the last to go, as if he had desired it all the time. "Good night, old sport...Good night to you as well, Dash."

But as Nick and I walked down the steps, I saw that the evening was not quite over. Fifty feet from the door, a dozen headlights illuminated a bizarre and tumultuous scene. In the ditch beside the road, right side up but violently shorn of one wheel, rested a new coupé which had left Gatsby's drive not two minutes before. The sharp jut of a wall accounted for the detachment of the wheel, which was now getting considerable attention from half a dozen curious chauffeurs. However, as they had left their cars blocking the road, a harsh discordant din from those in the rear had been audible for some time and added to the already violent confusion of the scene.

A man in a long duster had dismounted from the wreck and now stood in the middle of the road, looking from the car to the tire and from the tire to the observers in a pleasant, puzzled way.

"See!" he explained. "It went in the ditch."

The fact was infinitely astonishing to him—and I recognized first the unusual quality of wonder and then the man—it was the late patron of Gatsby's library.

"How'd it happen?"

He shrugged his shoulders.

"I know nothing whatever about mechanics," he said decisively.

"But how did it happen? Did you run into the wall?"

"Don't ask me," said Owl Eyes, washing his hands

of the whole matter. "I know very little about driving —next to nothing. It happened, and that's all I know."

"Well, if you're a poor driver you oughtn't to try driving at night."

"But I wasn't even trying," he explained indignantly. "I wasn't even trying."

An awed hush fell upon the bystanders.

"Do you want to commit suicide?"

"You're lucky it was just a wheel! A bad driver and not even trying!"

"You don't understand," explained the criminal. "I wasn't driving. There's another man in the car."

The shock that followed this declaration found voice in a sustained "Ah-h-h!" as the door of the coupé swung slowly open.

The crowd—it was now a crowd—stepped back involuntarily, and when the door had opened wide there was a ghostly pause. Then, very gradually, part by part, a pale dangling individual stepped out of the wreck, pawing tentatively at the ground with a large uncertain dancing shoe.

Blinded by the glare of the headlights, and confused by the incessant groaning of the horns, the apparition stood swaying for a moment before he perceived the man in the duster.

"Wha's matter?" he inquired calmly. "Did we run outa gas?"

"Look!"

Half a dozen fingers pointed at the amputated wheel—he stared at it for a moment and then looked upward as though he suspected that it had dropped from the sky.

"It came off," someone explained.

He nodded.

"At first I din' notice we'd stopped."

A pause. Then, taking a long breath and straightening his shoulders, he remarked in a determined voice: "Wonder'ff tell me where there's a gas'line station?"

At least a dozen men, some of them little better off than he was, explained to him that wheel and car were no longer joined by any physical bond.

"Back out," he suggested after a moment. "Put her in reverse."

"But the wheel's off!"

He hesitated.

"No harm in trying," he said.

The caterwauling horns had reached a crescendo and Nick and I turned away and cut across the lawn toward home.

I glanced back once. A wafer of a moon was shining over Gatsby's house, making the night fine as before and surviving the laughter and the sound of his still glowing garden. A sudden emptiness seemed to flow now from the windows and the great doors, endowing with complete isolation the figure of the host who stood on the porch, his hand up in a formal gesture of farewell.

Evaluating this report thus far, I feel a reader might be given the impression that the events of three separate nights several weeks apart were all that absorbed Nick and myself. On the contrary, they were merely casual events in a crowded summer and, until much later, they absorbed Nick infinitely less than his personal affairs. For me, they were merely memories.

Most of the time Nick worked. In the early morning, the sun threw his shadow westward as he hurried down the white chasms of lower New York to the Probity Trust. He knew the other clerks and young bond-salesmen by their first names and lunched with them in dark crowded restaurants on little pig sausages and mashed potatoes and coffee.

Nick even had a short affair with a girl who lived in Jersey City and worked in the accounting department. But, as I understand it, her brother began throwing mean looks in Nick's direction, so when she went on her vacation in July, he let it blow quietly away.

Nick and I took dinner usually at the Yale Club— for some reason it was the gloomiest event of our day —and then we went upstairs to the library, where he studied investments and securities for a conscientious hour; for my part, I merely napped. There were generally a few rioters around, but they never came into the library, so it was a good place for Nick to work and for me to sleep.

After that, if the night was mellow, we'd strolled down Madison Avenue past the old Murray Hill Hotel and over Thirty-third Street to the Pennsylvania Station.

Nick and I began to like New York, the racy, adventurous feel of it at night and the satisfaction that the constant flicker of men and women and dogs and machines gives to the restless eye. We liked to walk up Fifth Avenue and pick out romantic women from the crowd and imagine that in a few minutes we were going to enter into their lives, and no one would ever know or disapprove.

At the enchanted metropolitan twilight, we both felt a haunting loneliness sometimes, and felt it in others—poor young clerks who loitered in front of windows, waiting until it was time for a solitary restaurant dinner—young clerks in the dusk, wasting the most poignant moments of night and life.

Again at eight o'clock, when the dark lanes of the Forties were five deep with throbbing taxi cabs, bound for the theatre district, we'd sometimes feel a sinking in our hearts. Forms leaned together in the taxis as they waited, and voices sang, and there was laughter from unheard jokes, and lighted cigarettes outlined unintelligible gestures inside. Imagining that we, too, were hurrying toward gayety and sharing their intimate excitement, we wished them well.

For a while we lost sight of Jordan Baker, and then in midsummer we found her again. At first Nick was flattered to go places with her because she was a golf champion and everyone knew her name. Then it was something more. He wasn't actually in love, but I think Nick felt a sort of tender curiosity.

The bored haughty face that she turned to the world concealed something—most affectations conceal something eventually, even though they don't in the beginning—and one day we found what it was. When they were on a house-party together up in Warwick, she left a borrowed car out in the rain with the top down, and then lied about it—and suddenly I remembered the story about her that had eluded me that night at Daisy's. At her first big golf tournament, there was a row that nearly reached the newspapers—a suggestion that she had moved her ball from a bad lie in the semi-final round. The thing approached the proportions of a scandal—then died away. A caddy retracted his statement and the only other witness admitted that he might have been mistaken. The incident and the name had remained together in my mind and, I believe, in Nick's mind as well.

She was incurably dishonest. She wasn't able to endure being at a disadvantage, and given this unwillingness, I suppose she had begun dealing in subterfuges when she was very young, in order to keep that cool, insolent smile turned to the world and yet satisfy the demands of her hard jaunty body. She was like an unruly puppy who simply never matured, more by choice than nature.

It made no difference to Nick. Dishonesty in a woman is a thing he never blamed deeply—he was casually sorry, and then forgot. It was at that same house party that they had a curious conversation about driving a car. It started because she passed so close to some workmen that their fender flicked a button on one man's coat.

"You're a rotten driver," Nick protested. "Either you ought to be more careful or you oughtn't to drive at all."

"I am careful."

"No, you're not."

"Well, other people are," she said lightly.

"What's that got to do with it?"

"They'll keep out of my way," she insisted. "It takes two to make an accident."

"Suppose you met somebody just as careless as yourself."

"I hope I never will," she answered. "I hate careless people. That's why I like you."

Her grey, sun-strained eyes stared straight ahead, but she had deliberately shifted their relations, and I think—for a moment—Nick thought he loved her. But he was slow-thinking and full of interior rules that acted as brakes on his desires. And Nick knew that first he had to get himself definitely out of that tangle back home.

He'd been writing letters back home once a week and, after staring at the paper for a long moment, signing them: "Love, Nick."

But I know all he could think of was how, when that certain girl played tennis, a faint mustache of perspiration appeared on her upper lip. Nevertheless, there was a vague understanding that the relationship back home had to be tactfully broken off before Nick was free.

Here's what I've come to understand: Everyone believes they possess at least one of the cardinal virtues. And I suspect Nick considered himself one of the few truly honest people he had ever known.

Chapter Four

On Sunday morning, while church bells rang in the villages along shore, the world and its mistress returned to Gatsby's house and twinkled hilariously on his lawn.

"He's a bootlegger," said the young ladies, moving somewhere between his cocktails and his flowers. "One time he killed a man who had found out that he was nephew to von Hindenburg and second cousin to the devil. Reach me a rose, honey, and pour me a last drop into that there crystal glass."

Nick once wrote down on the empty spaces of a timetable the names of those who came to Gatsby's house that summer. It is an old timetable now, disintegrating at its folds and headed "This schedule in effect July 5th, 1922." But you can still read the grey names and they will give you a better impression than my generalities of those who accepted Gatsby's hospitality and paid him the subtle tribute of knowing nothing whatever about him.

From East Egg, then, came the Chester Beckers and the Leeches and a man named Bunsen whom Nick knew at Yale and Doctor Webster Civet who was drowned last summer up in Maine. And the Hornbeams and the Willie Voltaires and a whole clan named Blackbuck who always gathered in a corner and flipped up their noses like poodles at whosoever came near. And the Ismays and the Chrysties (or rather Hubert Auerbach and Mr. Chrystie's wife) and Edgar Beaver, whose hair they say turned cotton-white one winter afternoon for no good reason at all.

Clarence Endive was from East Egg, as I remember. He came only once, in white knickerbockers, and had a fight with a bum named Etty in the garden. From farther out on the Island came the Cheadles and the O. R. P. Schraeders and the Stonewall Jackson Abrams of Georgia and the Fishguards and the Ripley Snells. Snell was there three days before he went to the penitentiary, so drunk out on the gravel drive that Mrs. Ulysses Swett's automobile ran over his right hand. The Dancies came too and S. B. Whitebait, who was well over sixty, and Maurice A. Flink and the Hammerheads and Beluga the tobacco importer and Beluga's girls.

A man named Klipspringer was there so often and so long that he became known as "the boarder"—I doubt if he had any other home. Of theatrical people there were Gus Waize and Horace O'Donavan and Lester Meyer and George Duckweed and Francis Bull.

Also from New York were the Chromes and the Back-hyssons and the Dennickers and Russel Betty and the Corrigans and the Kellehers and the Dewars and the Scullys and S. W. Belcher and the Smirkes and the young Quinns, divorced now, and Henry L. Palmetto who killed himself by jumping in front of a subway train in Times Square.

Benny McClenahan arrived, always with four girls. They were never quite the same ones in physical person, but they were so identical—one with another—that it inevitably seemed they had been there before. I have forgotten their names—Jaqueline, I think, or else Consuela or Gloria or Judy or June. And their last names were either the melodious names of flowers and months or the sterner ones of the great American capitalists whose cousins, if pressed, they would confess themselves to be.

In addition to all these I can remember that Faustina O'Brien came there at least once and the Baedeker girls and young Brewer who had his nose shot off in the war and Mr. Albrucksburger and Miss Haag, his fiancée, and Ardita Fitz-Peters, and Mr. P. Jewett, once head of the American Legion, and Miss Claudia Hip with a man reputed to be her chauffeur, and a prince of something whom we called Duke and whose name, if I ever knew it, I have forgotten.

All these people came to Gatsby's house in the summer.

And not one of them had the common decency to bring a dog along. Except for my friend, Nick Carraway.

~

At nine o'clock, one morning late in July, Gatsby's gorgeous car lurched up the rocky drive to our door and gave out a burst of melody from its three noted horn. It was the first time he had called on us, though Nick and I had gone to two of his parties. Nick had even mounted in his hydroplane, and, at Gatsby's urgent invitation, both of us made frequent use of his beach. For a morning run, with sand pushing between your paws, there was nothing finer.

"Good morning, old sport, good morning, Dash. You're both having lunch with me today and I thought we'd ride up together."

He was balancing himself on the dashboard of his car with that resourcefulness of movement that is so peculiarly American—that comes, I suppose, with the absence of lifting work or rigid sitting in youth and, even more, with the formless grace of the nervous, sporadic games of humans. This quality was continually breaking through his punctilious manner in the shape of restlessness. He was never quite still; there was always a tapping foot somewhere or the impatient opening and closing of a hand. Like a dog who's tail never stops quivering, Gatsby was always in motion.

He saw Nick looking with admiration at his car.

"It's pretty, isn't it, old sport." He jumped off to give him a better view. "Haven't you ever seen it before?"

Nick had seen it. I had seen it. Everybody had seen it.

It was a rich cream color, bright with nickel, swollen here and there in its monstrous length with triumphant hatboxes and supper-boxes and toolboxes, and terraced with a labyrinth of windshields that mirrored a dozen suns. Sitting down behind many layers of glass in a sort of green leather conservatory, we started to town. As usual, I sat in the back, looking out a side window, enjoying the constantly moving view as it blurred past. While other dogs may have considered placing their heads out the open window, greyhounds don't do that. We never have.

Nick had talked with Gatsby perhaps half a dozen times in the past month and found, to our disappointment, that Gatsby had little to say. So, our first impression—that he was a person of some undefined consequence—had gradually faded and he had become simply the proprietor of an elaborate roadhouse next door.

And then came that disconcerting ride. We hadn't reached West Egg village before Gatsby began leaving his elegant sentences unfinished and slapping himself indecisively on the knee of his caramel-colored suit.

"Look here, old sport," he broke out surprisingly. "What's your opinion of me, anyhow?"

A little overwhelmed, Nick began the generalized evasions which that question deserves.

"Well, I'm going to tell you something about my life," Gatsby interrupted. "I don't want you to get a wrong idea of me from all these stories you hear."

So he was aware of the bizarre accusations that flavored conversation in his halls. I have excellent hearing, so of course I had heard them. But I was surprised Gatsby had heard them as well.

"I'll tell you God's truth." His right hand suddenly ordered divine retribution to stand by. "I am the son of some wealthy people in the middle-west—all dead now. I was brought up in America but educated at Oxford, because all my ancestors have been educated there for many years. It is a family tradition."

He looked at Nick sideways and then glanced at me in the rearview mirror—and I knew why Jordan Baker had believed he was lying. He hurried the phrase "educated at Oxford," or swallowed it or choked on it as though it had bothered him before. And with this doubt, his whole statement fell to pieces, and I wondered if there wasn't something a little sinister about him after all.

"What part of the middle-west?" Nick inquired casually. That was the exact question I would have asked.

"San Francisco."

"I see."

"My family all died, and I came into a good deal of money."

His voice was solemn, as if the memory of that sudden extinction of a clan still haunted him. For a moment I suspected that he was pulling our legs, but a glance at him convinced me otherwise.

"After that, I lived like a young rajah in all the capitals of Europe—Paris, Venice, Rome—collecting jewels, chiefly rubies, hunting big game, painting a little, things for myself only, and trying to forget something very sad that had happened to me long ago."

With what I could see was an effort, Nick managed to restrain incredulous laughter. The very phrases were worn so threadbare that they evoked no image except that of a turbaned "character" leaking sawdust at every pore as he pursued a tiger through the Bois de Boulogne.

"Then came the war, old sport. It was a great relief and I tried very hard to die, but I seemed to bear an enchanted life. I accepted a commission as first lieutenant when it began. In the Argonne Forest I took two machine-gun detachments so far forward that there was a half mile gap on either side of us where the infantry couldn't advance. We stayed there two days and two nights, a hundred and thirty men with sixteen Lewis guns. And when the infantry came up at last, they found the insignia of three German divisions among the piles of dead. I was promoted to be a major and every Allied government gave me a decoration—even Montenegro, little Montenegro down on the Adriatic Sea!"

Little Montenegro! He lifted up the words and nodded at them—with his smile. The smile comprehended Montenegro's troubled history and sympathized with the brave struggles of the Montenegrin people. My incredulity was submerged in fascination now; it was like skimming hastily through a dozen magazines.

He reached in his pocket and a piece of metal, slung on a ribbon, fell into Nick's palm.

"That's the one from Montenegro."

Nick held it up for closer inspection, giving me a clear view. To my astonishment, the thing had an authentic look. *Orderi di Danilo*, ran the circular legend, *Montenegro, Nicolas Rex.*

"Turn it."

"Major Jay Gatsby," Nick read. *"For Valour Extraordinary."*

"Here's another thing I always carry. A souvenir of Oxford days. It was taken in Trinity Quad—the man on my left is now the Earl of Dorcaster."

It was a photograph of half a dozen young men in blazers loafing in an archway through which were visible a host of spires. There was Gatsby, looking a little, not much, younger—with a cricket bat in his hand.

Then it was all true. I saw the skins of tigers flaming in his palace on the Grand Canal; I saw him opening a chest of rubies to ease, with their crimson-lighted depths, the gnawings of his broken heart.

"I'm going to make a big request of you two today," he said, pocketing his souvenirs with satisfaction, "so I thought you ought to know something about me. I didn't want you to think I was just some nobody. You see, I usually find myself among strangers, because I drift here and there trying to forget the sad thing that happened to me." He hesitated. "You'll hear about it this afternoon."

"At lunch?"

"No, this afternoon. I happened to find out that you're taking Miss Baker to tea."

"Do you mean you're in love with Miss Baker?"

"No, old sport, I'm not. But Miss Baker has kindly consented to speak to you about this matter."

I hadn't the faintest idea what "this matter" was, but I was more annoyed than interested. I know Nick hadn't asked Jordan to tea in order to discuss Mr. Jay Gatsby. I was sure the request would be something utterly fantastic and for a moment I was sorry I'd ever set a paw upon his overpopulated lawn.

He wouldn't say another word. His correctness grew on him as we neared the city. We passed Port Roosevelt, where there was a glimpse of red-belted ocean-going ships, and sped along a cobbled slum lined with the dark, undeserted saloons of the faded gilt nineteen-hundreds. Then the valley of ashes opened out on both sides of us, and I had a glimpse of Mrs. Wilson straining at the garage pump with panting vitality as we went by.

With fenders spread like wings, we scattered light through half Astoria—only half, for as we twisted among the pillars of the elevated, I heard the familiar "jug—jug—*spat*!" of a motorcycle, and a frantic policeman rode alongside.

"All right, old sport," called Gatsby. We slowed down. Taking a white card from his wallet, he waved it before the man's eyes.

"Right you are," agreed the policeman, tipping his cap. "Know you next time, Mr. Gatsby. Excuse *me*!"

"What was that?" Nick inquired. "The picture of Oxford?"

"I was able to do the commissioner a favor once, and he sends me a Christmas card every year."

Over the great bridge, with the sunlight through the girders making a constant flicker upon the moving cars, with the city rising up across the river in white heaps and sugar lumps all built with a wish out of non-olfactory money. The city seen from the Queensboro Bridge is always the city seen for the first time, in its first wild promise of all the mystery and the beauty in the world.

A dead man passed us in a hearse heaped with blooms, followed by two carriages with drawn blinds and by more cheerful carriages for friends. The friends looked out at us with the tragic eyes and short upper lips of south-eastern Europe, and I was glad that the sight of Gatsby's splendid car was included in their somber holiday.

"Anything can happen now that we've slid over this bridge," I thought. "Anything at all..."

Even Gatsby could happen, without any particular wonder.

Roaring noon. In a well-fanned Forty-second Street cellar, we met Gatsby for lunch. Blinking away the brightness of the street outside, my eyes picked him out obscurely in the anteroom, talking to another man. I led Nick in that direction, as his eyes were still adjusting.

"Mr. Carraway this is my friend Mr. Wolfsheim."

A small, flat-nosed man raised his large head and regarded us with two fine growths of hair which luxuriated in either nostril. After a moment I discovered his tiny eyes in the half darkness.

"—so, I took one look at him—" said Mr. Wolfsheim, shaking Nick's hand earnestly, "—and what do you think I did?"

"What?" Nick inquired politely.

But evidently he was not addressing Nick, for he dropped his hand and turned to Gatsby.

"I handed the money to Katspaugh and I said, 'All right, Katspaugh, don't pay him a penny till he shuts his mouth.' He shut it then and there."

Gatsby moved us forward into the restaurant, whereupon Mr. Wolfsheim swallowed a new sentence he was starting and lapsed into a somnambulatory abstraction.

"Highballs?" asked the head waiter.

"This is a nice restaurant here," said Mr. Wolfsheim, looking at the Presbyterian nymphs on the ceiling. "But I like across the street better!"

"Yes, highballs," agreed Gatsby, and then to Mr. Wolfsheim: "It's too hot over there."

"Hot and small—yes," said Mr. Wolfsheim. "But full of memories."

"What place is that?" Nick asked.

"The old Metropole."

"The old Metropole," brooded Mr. Wolfsheim gloomily. "Filled with faces dead and gone. Filled with friends gone now forever. I can't forget so long as I live the night they shot Rosy Rosenthal there. It was six of us at the table and Rosy had eat and drunk a lot all evening. When it was almost morning, the waiter came up to him with a funny look and says somebody wants to speak to him outside. 'All right,' says Rosy and begins to get up and I pulled him down in his chair. 'Let the bastards come in here if they want you, Rosy, but don't you, so help me, move outside this room.' It was four o'clock in the morning then, and if we'd of raised the blinds we'd of seen daylight."

"Did he go?" Nick asked innocently.

"Sure he went." Mr. Wolfsheim's eyes flashed at Nick indignantly. "He turned around in the door and says, 'Don't let that waiter take away my coffee!' Then he went out on the sidewalk and they shot him three times in his full belly and drove away."

"Four of them were electrocuted," Nick said. I remembered hearing of it as well.

"Five with Becker." Mr. Wolfsheim turned to Nick in an interested way. He had yet to glance down at me even once. Perhaps he hadn't seen me yet. "I understand you're looking for a business gonnegtion."

The juxtaposition of these two remarks was startling. Gatsby answered for Nick.

"Oh, no," he exclaimed. "This isn't the man!"

"No?" Mr. Wolfsheim seemed disappointed.

"These are just friends. I told you we'd talk about that some other time."

"I beg your pardon," said Mr. Wolfsheim. "I had a wrong man."

A succulent hash arrived, and Mr. Wolfsheim, forgetting the more sentimental atmosphere of the old

Metropole, began to eat with ferocious delicacy, like a starving cat. His eyes, meanwhile, roved very slowly all around the room—he completed the arc by turning to inspect the people directly behind.

"Look here, old sport," said Gatsby, leaning toward Nick. "I'm afraid I made you a little angry this morning in the car."

There was the smile again, but this time I could feel Nick holding out against it.

"I don't like mysteries," Nick answered. "And I don't understand why you won't come out frankly and tell me what you want. Why has it all got to come through Miss Baker?"

"Oh, it's nothing underhanded," he assured us. "Miss Baker's a great sportswoman, you know, and she'd never do anything that wasn't all right."

Suddenly he looked at his watch, jumped up and hurried from the room, leaving us with Mr. Wolfsheim at the table.

"He has to telephone," said Mr. Wolfsheim, following him with his eyes. "Fine fellow, isn't he? Handsome to look at and a perfect gentleman."

"Yes."

"He's an Oggsford man."

"Oh!"

"He went to Oggsford College in England. You know Oggsford College?"

"I've heard of it."

"It's one of the most famous colleges in the world."

"Have you known Gatsby for a long time?" Nick inquired.

"Several years," he answered in a gratified way. "I made the pleasure of his acquaintance just after the war. But I knew I had discovered a man of fine breeding after I talked with him an hour. I said to myself: 'There's the kind of man you'd like to take home and introduce to your mother and sister.'" He paused and glanced down at me for what felt like the first time. "I see you're looking at my cuff buttons."

I hadn't been looking at them, but I did now. They were composed of oddly familiar pieces of ivory. Nick looked as well.

"Finest specimens of human molars," he informed us.

"Well!" Nick inspected them. "That's a very interesting idea."

"Yeah." He flipped his sleeves up under his coat. "Yeah, Gatsby's very careful about women. He would never so much as look at a friend's wife."

When the subject of this instinctive trust returned to the table and sat down, Mr. Wolfsheim drank his coffee with a jerk and got to his feet.

"I have enjoyed my lunch," he said. "And I'm going to run off from you three youngsters before I outstay my welcome."

"Don't hurry, Meyer," said Gatsby, without enthusiasm. Mr. Wolfsheim raised his hand in a sort of benediction.

"You're very polite but I belong to another generation," he announced solemnly. "You sit here and discuss your sports and your young ladies and your—" He supplied an imaginary noun with another wave of his hand. "As for me, I am fifty years old, and I won't impose myself on you any longer."

As he shook hands and patted my head and turned away, it seemed like he was trembling. I wondered if Nick had said anything to offend him.

"He becomes very sentimental sometimes," explained Gatsby. "This is one of his sentimental days. He's quite a character around New York—a denizen of Broadway."

"Who is he anyhow—an actor?"

"No."

"A dentist?"

"Meyer Wolfsheim? No, he's a gambler." Gatsby hesitated, then added coolly: "He's the man who fixed the World's Series back in 1919."

"Fixed the World's Series?" Nick repeated.

The idea staggered me. I remembered of course that the World's Series had been fixed in 1919, but if I had thought of it at all, I would have thought of it as a thing that merely *happened*, the end of some inevitable chain. It never occurred to me that one human could start to play with the faith of fifty million people—with the single-mindedness of a burglar blowing a safe.

"How did he happen to do that?" Nick asked after a minute.

"He just saw the opportunity."

"Why isn't he in jail?"

"They can't get him, old sport. He's a smart man."

Nick insisted on paying the check. As the waiter brought his change, we both caught sight of Tom Buchanan across the crowded room.

"Come along with me for a minute," Nick said. "I've got to say hello to someone."

When he saw us, Tom jumped up and took half a dozen steps in our direction.

"Where've you been?" he demanded eagerly. "Daisy's furious because you haven't called up."

"This is Mr. Gatsby, Mr. Buchanan."

They shook hands briefly and a strained, unfamiliar look of embarrassment came over Gatsby's face.

"How've you been, anyhow?" demanded Tom of Nick. "How'd you happen to come up this far to eat?"

"I've been having lunch with Mr. Gatsby."

Nick turned toward Mr. Gatsby, but he was no longer there.

One October day in nineteen-seventeen—(said Jordan Baker that afternoon, sitting up very straight on a straight chair in the tea-garden at the Plaza Hotel)—I was walking along from one place to another, half on the sidewalks and half on the lawns. I was happier on the lawns because I had on shoes from England with rubber nobs on the soles that bit into the soft ground. I had on a new plaid skirt also that blew a little in the wind and whenever this happened the red, white and blue banners in front of all the houses stretched out stiff and said tut-tut-tut-tut in a disapproving way.

The largest of the banners and the largest of the lawns belonged to Daisy Fay's house. She was just eighteen, two years older than me, and by far the most popular of all the young girls in Louisville. She dressed in white and had a little white roadster and all day long the telephone rang in her house and excited young officers from Camp Taylor demanded the privilege of monopolizing her that night, "anyways, for an hour!"

When I came opposite her house that morning, her white roadster was beside the curb, and she was sitting in it with a lieutenant I had never seen before. They were so engrossed in each other that she didn't see me until I was five feet away.

"Hello Jordan," she called unexpectedly. "Please come here."

I was flattered that she wanted to speak to me, because of all the older girls, I admired her most. She asked me if I was going to the Red Cross and make bandages. I was. Well, then, would I tell them that she couldn't come that day? The officer looked at Daisy while she was speaking, in a way that every young girl wants to be looked at sometime, and because it seemed romantic to me I have remembered the incident ever since. His name was Jay Gatsby and I didn't lay eyes on him again for over four years—even after I'd met him on Long Island, I didn't realize it was the same man.

That was nineteen-seventeen. By the next year I had a few beaux myself, and I began to play in tournaments, so I didn't see Daisy very often. She went with a slightly older crowd—when she went with anyone at all. Wild rumors were circulating about her—how her mother had found her packing her bag one winter night to go to New York and say goodbye to a soldier who was going overseas. She was effectually prevented, but she wasn't on speaking terms with her family for several weeks. After that, she didn't play around with the soldiers anymore but only with a few flat-footed, short-sighted young men in town who couldn't get into the army at all.

By the next autumn she was gay again, gay as ever. She had a debut after the Armistice, and in February she was presumably engaged to a man from New Orleans. In June she married Tom Buchanan of Chicago with more pomp and circumstance than Louisville ever knew before. He came down with a hundred people in four private cars and hired a whole floor of the Seelbach Hotel, and the day before the wedding he gave her a string of pearls valued at three hundred and fifty thousand dollars.

I was bridesmaid. I came into her room half an hour before the bridal dinner and found her lying on her bed as lovely as the June night in her flowered dress—and as drunk as a monkey. She had a bottle of sauterne in one hand and a letter in the other.

"'Gratulate me," she muttered. "Never had a drink before but oh, how I do enjoy it."

"What's the matter, Daisy?"

I was scared, I can tell you; I'd never seen a girl like that before.

"Here, dearies." She groped around in a wastebasket she had with her on the bed and pulled out the string of pearls. "Take 'em downstairs and give 'em back to whoever they belong to. Tell 'em all Daisy's change' her mine. Say 'Daisy's change' her mine!'."

She began to cry—she cried and cried. I rushed out and found her mother's maid and we locked the door and got her into a cold bath. She wouldn't let go of the letter. She took it into the tub with her and squeezed it up into a wet ball, and only let me leave it in the soap dish when she saw that it was coming to pieces like snow.

But she didn't say another word. We gave her spirits of ammonia and put ice on her forehead and hooked her back into her dress and half an hour later when we walked out of the room the pearls were around her neck and the incident was over. Next day at five o'clock she married Tom Buchanan without so much as a shiver and started off on a three months' trip to the South Seas.

I saw them in Santa Barbara when they came back and I thought I'd never seen a girl so mad about her husband. If he left the room for a minute she'd look around uneasily and say "Where's Tom gone?" and wear the most abstracted expression until she saw him coming in the door. She used to sit on the sand with his head in her lap by the hour, rubbing her fingers over his eyes and looking at him with unfathomable delight. It was touching to see them together—it made you laugh in a hushed, fascinated way. That was in August. A week after I left Santa Barbara, Tom ran into a wagon on the Ventura road one night and ripped a front wheel off his car. The girl who was with him got into the papers too because her arm was broken—she was one of the chambermaids in the Santa Barbara Hotel.

The next April, Daisy had her little girl and they went to France for a year. I saw them one spring in Cannes and later in Deauville and then they came back to Chicago to settle down. Daisy was popular in Chicago, as you know. They moved with a fast crowd, all of them young and rich and wild, but she came out with an absolutely perfect reputation. Perhaps because she doesn't drink. It's a great advantage not to drink among hard-drinking people. You can hold your tongue and, moreover, you can time any little irregularity of your own so that everybody else is so blind that they don't see or care. Perhaps Daisy never went in for amour at all—and yet there's something in that voice of hers...

Well, about six weeks ago, she heard the name Gatsby for the first time in years. It was when I asked you—do you remember?—if you knew Gatsby in West Egg. After you had gone home, she came into my room and woke me up, and said, "What Gatsby?" And when I described him—I was half asleep—she said *in the strangest voice that it must be the man she used to know. It wasn't until then that I connected this Gatsby with the officer in her white car.*

When Jordan Baker had finished telling all this we had left the Plaza for half an hour and were driving in a Victoria through Central Park. The sun had gone down behind the tall apartments of the movie stars in the West Fifties, and the clear voices of girls—already gathered like crickets on the grass—rose through the hot twilight:

I'm the Sheik of Araby,
Your love belongs to me.
At night when you're asleep,
Into your tent I'll creep—

"It was a strange coincidence," Nick said.

"But it wasn't a coincidence at all."

"Why not?"

"Gatsby bought that house so that Daisy would be just across the bay."

Then it had not been merely the stars to which he had aspired on that June night. He came alive to me, delivered suddenly from the womb of his purposeless splendor.

"He wants to know—" continued Jordan, "—if you'll invite Daisy to your house some afternoon and then let him come over."

I could tell the modesty of the demand shook Nick. Gatsby had waited five years and bought a mansion where he dispensed starlight to casual moths so that he could "come over" some afternoon to a stranger's garden.

"Did I have to know all this before he could ask such a little thing?"

"He's afraid. He's waited so long. He thought you might be offended. You see he's a regular tough underneath it all."

Something worried Nick.

"Why didn't he ask you to arrange a meeting?"

"He wants her to see his house," she explained. "And your house is right next door."

"Oh!"

"I think he half expected her to wander into one of his parties, some night, but she never did," Jordan continued. "Then he began asking people casually if they knew her, and I was the first one he found. It was that night he sent for me at his dance, and you should have heard the elaborate way he worked up to it. Of course, I immediately suggested a luncheon in New York—and I thought he'd go mad: 'I don't want to do anything out of the way!' he kept saying. 'I want to see her right next door.'

"When I said you were a particular friend of Tom's, he started to abandon the whole idea. He doesn't know very much about Tom, though he says he's read a Chicago paper for years just on the chance of catching a glimpse of Daisy's name."

It was dark now, and as we dipped under a little bridge, Nick put his arm around Jordan's golden shoulder and drew her toward him and asked her to dinner. I could tell he wasn't thinking of Daisy and Gatsby anymore, but of this clean, hard, limited person who dealt in universal skepticism and who leaned back jauntily just within the circle of his arm.

A phrase began to beat in my ears with a sort of heady excitement: "There are only the pursued, the pursuing, the busy and the tired." I have run races, I have lost races, and I have sat them out as well. I understood the sentiment.

"And Daisy ought to have something in her life," murmured Jordan to Nick.

"Does she want to see Gatsby?"

"She's not to know about it. Gatsby doesn't want her to know. You're just supposed to invite her to tea."

We passed a barrier of dark trees, and then the facade of Fifty-ninth Street, a block of delicate pale light, beamed down into the park.

Unlike Gatsby and Tom Buchanan, Nick had no girl whose disembodied face floated along the dark cornices and blinding signs. And so he drew up the girl beside him, tightening his arms. Her wan, scornful mouth smiled and so he drew her up again, closer, this time to his face.

When we came home to West Egg that night, I was afraid for a moment that our house was on fire. Two o'clock and the whole corner of the peninsula was blazing with light, which fell unreal on the shrubbery and made thin elongating glints upon the roadside wires. Turning a corner, I saw that it was Gatsby's house, lit from tower to cellar.

At first I thought it was another party, a wild rout that had resolved itself into "hide-and-go-seek" or "sardines-in-the-box," with all the house thrown open to the game. But there wasn't a sound. Only wind in the trees which blew the wires and made the lights go off and on again as if the house had winked into the darkness. As our taxi groaned away, I saw Gatsby walking toward us across his lawn.

"Your place looks like the world's fair," Nick said.

"Does it?" He turned his eyes toward it absently. "I

have been glancing into some of the rooms. Let's go to Coney Island, old sport. In my car."

"It's too late."

"Well, suppose we take a plunge in the swimming pool? I haven't made use of it all summer."

"We've got to go to bed."

"All right."

He waited, looking at us with suppressed eagerness.

"I talked with Miss Baker," Nick said after a moment. "I'm going to call up Daisy tomorrow and invite her over here to tea."

"Oh, that's all right," he said carelessly. "I don't want to put you to any trouble."

"What day would suit you?"

"What day would suit *you*?" he corrected Nick quickly. "I don't want to put you to any trouble, you see."

"How about the day after tomorrow?"

He considered for a moment. Then, with reluctance:

"I want to get the grass cut," he said.

We all looked at the grass—there was a sharp line where our ragged lawn ended and the darker, well-kept expanse of his began. I supposed that he meant our lawn. Personally, I saw no need to cut our grass; I love the feel of long, unkempt blades of grass between my paws during a morning run. But, as I suspected from the beginning, my taste was not that of Gatsby's.

"There's another little thing," he said uncertainly, and hesitated.

"Would you rather put it off for a few days?" Nick asked.

"Oh, it isn't about that. At least—" He fumbled with a series of beginnings. "Why, I thought—why, look here, old sport, you don't make much money, do you?"

"Not very much."

This seemed to reassure him, and he continued more confidently.

"I thought you didn't, if you'll pardon my—you see, I carry on a little business on the side, a sort of sideline, you understand. And I thought that if you don't make very much—You're selling bonds, aren't you, old sport?"

"Trying to."

"Well, this would interest you. It wouldn't take up much of your time and you might pick up a nice bit of money. It happens to be a rather confidential sort of thing."

I realize now that under different circumstances that conversation might have been one of the crises of Nick's life. But, because the offer was obviously and tactlessly for a service to be rendered, I think Nick had no choice except to cut him off there.

"I've got my hands full," Nick said. "I'm much obliged, but I couldn't take on any more work."

Gatsby waited a moment longer, hoping—I think —for Nick to begin a conversation. But Nick was too absorbed to be responsive, so Gatsby went unwillingly home.

∽

The evening had made Nick light-headed and happy; I think he walked into a deep sleep as we entered our front door. For my part, I didn't know whether or not Gatsby went to Coney Island or for how many hours he "glanced into rooms" while his house blazed gaudily on. I thought no more about it and, like Nick, quickly fell asleep.

The next morning, Nick called up Daisy from the office and invited her to come to tea. From my position at his feet, I could clearly hear both sides of the conversation.

"Don't bring Tom," he warned her.

"What?"

"Don't bring Tom."

"Who is 'Tom'?" she asked innocently.

The day agreed upon was pouring rain. At eleven o'clock, a man in a raincoat dragging a lawnmower tapped at our front door and said that Mr. Gatsby had sent him over to cut our grass. This reminded Nick that he had forgotten to tell our silent Finnish woman —who prepared meals and kept house—to come back. So, we drove into West Egg Village to search for her among soggy, white-washed alleys and to buy some cups and lemons and flowers.

The flowers were unnecessary, for at two o'clock a greenhouse arrived from Gatsby's, with innumerable receptacles to contain it. An hour later the front door opened nervously, and Gatsby in a white flannel suit, silver shirt and gold-colored tie hurried in. He was pale and there were dark signs of sleeplessness beneath his eyes.

"Is everything all right?" he asked immediately.

"The grass looks fine, if that's what you mean."

"What grass?" he inquired blankly. "Oh, the grass in the yard." He looked out the window at it, but judging from his expression I don't believe he saw a thing.

"Looks very good," he remarked vaguely. "One of the papers said they thought the rain would stop about four. I think it was 'The Journal.' Have you got everything you need in the shape of—of tea?"

We took him into the pantry where he looked a little reproachfully at the Finn. Together we scrutinized the twelve lemon cakes from the delicatessen shop.

"Will they do?" Nick asked.

"Of course, of course! They're fine!" and he added hollowly, "...old sport."

The rain cooled about half-past three to a damp mist through which occasional thin drops swam like dew. Gatsby looked with vacant eyes through a copy of Clay's "Economics," peering toward the bleared windows from time to time as if a series of invisible but alarming happenings were taking place outside. Finally, he got up and informed us in an uncertain voice that he was going home.

"Why's that?"

"Nobody's coming to tea. It's too late!" He looked at his watch as if there was some pressing demand on his time elsewhere. "I can't wait all day."

"Don't be silly; it's just two minutes to four."

He sat down, miserably, as if Nick had pushed him, and simultaneously there was the sound of a motor turning into our lane. We all jumped up and, a little harrowed myself, Nick and I went out into the yard.

Under the dripping bare lilac trees a large open car was coming up the drive. It stopped. Daisy's face, tipped sideways beneath a three-cornered lavender hat, looked out at us with a bright ecstatic smile.

"Is this absolutely where you live, my dearest one?"

The exhilarating ripple of her voice was a wild tonic in the rain. I had to follow the sound of it for a moment, up and down, with my ear alone before any words came through. A damp streak of hair lay like a dash of blue paint across her cheek and her hand was wet with glistening drops as Nick helped her from the car.

"Are you in love with me," she said low in his ear. "Or why did I have to come alone?"

"That's the secret of Castle Rackrent. Tell your chauffeur to go far away and spend an hour."

"Come back in an hour, Ferdie." Then in a grave murmur, "His name is Ferdie."

"Does the gasoline affect his nose?"

"I don't think so," she said innocently. "Why?"

We went in. To my overwhelming surprise the living room was deserted.

"Well, that's funny!" Nick exclaimed.

"What's funny?"

She turned her head as there was a light, dignified knocking at the front door. Nick went out and opened it. Gatsby, pale as death, with his hands plunged like weights in his coat pockets, was standing in a puddle of water glaring tragically into Nick's eyes.

With his hands still in his coat pockets he stalked by me into the hall, turned sharply as if he were on a wire and disappeared into the living room. It wasn't a bit funny. Aware of the loud beating of my own heart, I watched as Nick pulled the door against the increasing rain.

For half a minute there wasn't a sound. Then from the living room I heard a sort of choking murmur and part of a laugh, followed by Daisy's voice on a clear artificial note.

"I certainly am awfully glad to see you again."

A pause; it endured horribly. I had nothing to do in the hall, so I went into the room. Nick followed me.

Gatsby, his hands still in his pockets, was reclining against the mantelpiece in a strained counterfeit of perfect ease, even of boredom. His head leaned back so far that it rested against the face of a defunct mantelpiece clock. From this position, his distraught eyes stared down at Daisy, who was sitting frightened but graceful on the edge of a stiff chair.

"We've met before," muttered Gatsby. His eyes glanced momentarily at us and his lips parted with an abortive attempt at a laugh. Luckily the clock took this moment to tilt dangerously at the pressure of his head, whereupon he turned and caught it with trembling fingers and set it back in place. Then he sat down, rigidly, his elbow on the arm of the sofa and his chin in his hand.

"I'm sorry about the clock," he said.

Nick's own face had now assumed a deep tropical burn. I couldn't muster up a single commonplace thought out of the thousand in my head. Nick had more luck than I, but not much.

"It's an old clock," he told them idiotically.

I think we all believed for a moment that it had smashed in pieces on the floor.

"We haven't met for many years," said Daisy, her voice as matter of fact as it could ever be.

"Five years next November."

The automatic quality of Gatsby's answer set us all back at least another minute. Nick got them both on their feet with the desperate suggestion that they help him make tea in the kitchen, when the demoniac Finn brought it in on a tray.

Amid the welcome confusion of cups and cakes, a certain physical decency established itself. Gatsby got himself into a shadow and, while Daisy and Nick talked, looked conscientiously from one to the other of them with tense unhappy eyes. He glanced down in my direction, and I made every effort to return a comforting gaze. However, as calmness wasn't an end in itself, Nick made an excuse at the first possible moment and got to his feet.

"Where are you going?" demanded Gatsby in immediate alarm.

"I'll be back."

"I've got to speak to you about something before you go."

He followed us wildly into the kitchen, closed the door and whispered: "Oh, God!" in a miserable way.

"What's the matter?"

"This is a terrible mistake," he said, shaking his head from side to side. "A terrible, terrible mistake."

"You're just embarrassed, that's all," Nick said, and luckily he added: "Daisy's embarrassed too."

"She's embarrassed?" he repeated incredulously.

"Just as much as you are."

"Don't talk so loud."

"You're acting like a little boy," Nick broke out impatiently. "Not only that, but you're rude. Daisy's sitting in there, all alone."

He raised his hand to stop Nick's words, looked at him with unforgettable reproach and—opening the door cautiously—went back into the other room.

Nick and I walked out the back way—just as Gatsby had when he had made his nervous circuit of the house half an hour before—and we ran for a huge black knotted tree whose massed leaves made a fabric against the rain. Once more it was pouring and our irregular lawn, well-shaved by Gatsby's gardener, abounded in small muddy swamps and prehistoric marshes. The quick run in the rain helped to break the awkward spell which had overtaken me in the house. It felt good to run.

There was nothing to look at from under the tree except Gatsby's enormous house, so we stared at it for half an hour.

After half an hour the sun shone again and the grocer's automobile rounded Gatsby's drive with the raw material for his servants' dinner—I felt sure he wouldn't eat a spoonful. A maid began opening the upper windows of his house, appeared momentarily in each, and, leaning from a large central bay, spat meditatively into the garden. It was time we went back. While the rain continued it had seemed like the murmur of their voices, rising and swelling a little, now and then, with gusts of emotion. But in the new silence I felt that silence had fallen within the house too.

We went in—after making every possible noise in the kitchen short of pushing over the stove—but I don't believe they heard a sound. They were sitting at either end of the couch looking at each other as if some question had been asked or was in the air, and every vestige of embarrassment was gone.

Daisy's face was smeared with tears and when we came in, she jumped up and began wiping at it with her handkerchief before a mirror. But there was a change in Gatsby that was simply confounding. He literally glowed; without a word or a gesture of exultation, a new well-being radiated from him and filled the little room.

"Oh, hello, old sport, hello Dash," he said, as if he hadn't seen us for years. I thought for a moment he was going to shake hands.

"It's stopped raining."

"Has it?" When he realized what Nick was talking about, that there were twinkle-bells of sunshine in the room, he smiled like a weather man, like an ecstatic patron of recurrent light, and repeated the news to Daisy. "What do you think of that? It's stopped raining."

"I'm glad, Jay." Her throat, full of aching, grieving beauty, told only of her unexpected joy.

"I want you and Dash and Daisy to come over to my house," he said. "I'd like to show her around."

"You're sure you want us to come?"

"Absolutely, old sport."

Daisy went upstairs to wash her face—too late I thought with humiliation of Nick's towels—while Gatsby and Nick and I waited on the lawn.

"My house looks well, doesn't it?" he demanded. "See how the whole front of it catches the light."

Nick agreed that it was splendid.

"Yes." His eyes went over it, every arched door and square tower. "It took me just three years to earn the money that bought it."

"I thought you inherited your money."

"I did, old sport," he said automatically, "but I lost most of it in the big panic—the panic of the war."

I think he hardly knew what he was saying, for when Nick asked him what business he was in he answered. "That's my affair," before he realized that it wasn't the appropriate reply.

"Oh, I've been in several things," he corrected himself. "I was in the drug business and then I was in the oil business. But I'm not in either one now." He looked at us with more attention, going so far as to reach down and affectionately pat my head. "Do you mean you've been thinking over what I proposed the other night?"

Before Nick could answer, Daisy came out of the

house and two rows of brass buttons on her dress gleamed in the sunlight.

"That huge place *there*?" she cried pointing.

"Do you like it?"

"I love it, but I don't see how you live there all alone."

"I keep it always full of interesting people, night and day. People who do interesting things. Celebrated people."

Instead of taking the short cut along the Sound, we went down the road and entered by the big postern. With enchanting murmurs, Daisy admired this aspect or that of the feudal silhouette against the sky, admired the gardens, the sparkling odor of jonquils and the frothy odor of hawthorn and plum blossoms and the pale gold odor of kiss-me-at-the-gate. It was strange to reach the marble steps and find no stir of bright dresses in and out the door and hear no sound but bird voices in the trees.

And inside, as we wandered through Marie Antoinette music rooms and Restoration salons, I felt that there were guests concealed behind every couch and table, under orders to be breathlessly silent until we had passed through. As Gatsby closed the door of "the Merton College Library," I could have sworn I heard the owl-eyed man break into ghostly laughter.

We went upstairs, through period bedrooms swathed in rose and lavender silk and vivid with new flowers, through dressing rooms and poolrooms, and bathrooms with sunken baths—intruding into one chamber where a disheveled man in pajamas was doing liver exercises on the floor. It was Mr. Klipspringer, the "boarder." I had seen him wandering hungrily about the beach that morning. Finally, we came to Gatsby's own apartment, a bedroom and a bath and an Adam study, where the humans sat down and drank a glass of some Chartreuse he took from a cupboard in the wall.

He hadn't once ceased looking at Daisy and I think he revalued everything in his house according to the measure of response it drew from her well-loved eyes. Sometimes, too, he stared around at his possessions in a dazed way as though in her actual and astounding presence none of it was any longer real. Once he nearly toppled down a flight of stairs.

His bedroom was the simplest room of all—except where the dresser was garnished with a toilet set of pure dull gold. Daisy took the brush with delight and smoothed her hair, whereupon Gatsby sat down and shaded his eyes and began to laugh.

"It's the funniest thing, old sport," he said hilariously. "I can't—when I try to—"

He had passed visibly through two states and was entering upon a third. After his embarrassment and his unreasoning joy, he was consumed with wonder at her presence. He had been full of the idea so long, dreamed it right through to the end, waited with his teeth set, so to speak, at an inconceivable pitch of intensity. Now, in the reaction, he was running down like an overwound clock.

Recovering himself in a minute, he opened for us two hulking patent cabinets which held his massed suits and dressing-gowns and ties, and his shirts, piled like bricks in stacks a dozen high.

"I've got a man in England who buys me clothes. He sends over a selection of things at the beginning of each season, spring and fall."

He took out a pile of shirts and began throwing them, one by one before us, shirts of sheer linen and thick silk and fine flannel which lost their folds as they fell and covered the table in many-colored disarray.

While we admired, he brought more and the soft rich heap mounted higher—shirts with stripes and scrolls and plaids in coral and apple-green and lavender and faint orange with monograms of Indian blue. Suddenly with a strained sound, Daisy bent her head into the shirts and began to cry stormily.

"They're such beautiful shirts," she sobbed, her voice muffled in the thick folds. "It makes me sad because I've never seen such—such beautiful shirts before."

After the house, we were to see the grounds and the swimming pool, and the hydroplane and the midsummer flowers—but outside Gatsby's window it began to rain again, so we stood in a row looking at the corrugated surface of the Sound.

"If it wasn't for the mist, we could see your home across the bay," said Gatsby. "You always have a green light that burns all night at the end of your dock."

Daisy put her arm through his abruptly, but he

seemed absorbed in what he had just said. Possibly it had occurred to him that the colossal significance of that light had now vanished forever. Compared to the great distance that had separated him from Daisy, it had seemed very near to her, almost touching her. It had seemed as close as a star to the moon. Now it was again a green light on a dock. His count of enchanted objects had diminished by one.

Nick and I began to walk about the room, examining various indefinite objects in the half darkness. A large photograph of an elderly man in yachting costume attracted us, hung on the wall over his desk.

"Who's this?"

"That? That's Mr. Dan Cody, old sport."

The name sounded faintly familiar.

"He's dead now. He used to be my best friend years ago."

There was a small picture of Gatsby, also in yachting costume, on the bureau—Gatsby with his head thrown back defiantly—taken apparently when he was about eighteen.

"I adore it!" exclaimed Daisy. "The pompadour! You never told me you had a pompadour—or a yacht."

"Look at this," said Gatsby quickly. "Here's a lot of clippings—about you."

They stood side by side examining it. When the phone rang, Gatsby took up the receiver.

"Yes...Well, I can't talk now...I can't talk now, old sport...I said a *small* town...He must know what a small town is...Well, he's no use to us if Detroit is his idea of a small town..."

He rang off.

"Come here *quick*!" cried Daisy at the window.

The rain was still falling, but the darkness had parted in the west, and there was a pink and golden billow of foamy clouds above the sea.

"Look at that," she whispered, and then after a moment: "I'd like to just get one of those pink clouds and put you in it and push you around."

Nick and I tried to go then, but they wouldn't hear of it; perhaps our presence made them feel more satisfactorily alone.

"I know what we'll do," said Gatsby, "we'll have Klipspringer play the piano."

He went out of the room calling "Ewing!" and returned in a few minutes accompanied by an embarrassed, slightly worn young man with shell-rimmed glasses and scanty blonde hair. He was now decently clothed in a "sport shirt" open at the neck, sneakers and duck trousers of a nebulous hue.

"Did we interrupt your exercises?" inquired Daisy politely.

"I was asleep," cried Mr. Klipspringer, in a spasm of embarrassment. "That is, I'd *been* asleep. Then I got up..."

"Klipspringer plays the piano," said Gatsby, cutting him off. "Don't you, Ewing, old sport?"

"I don't play well. I don't—I hardly play at all. I'm all out of prac—"

"We'll go downstairs," interrupted Gatsby. He flipped a switch. The grey windows disappeared as the house glowed full of light.

In the music room Gatsby turned on a solitary lamp beside the piano. He lit Daisy's cigarette from a trembling match and sat down with her on a couch far across the room where there was no light save what the gleaming floor bounced in from the hall.

When Klipspringer had played "The Love Nest," he turned around on the bench and searched unhappily for Gatsby in the gloom.

"I'm all out of practice, you see. I told you I couldn't play. I'm all out of prac—"

"Don't talk so much, old sport," commanded Gatsby. "Play!"

In the morning,
In the evening,
Ain't we got fun—

Outside the wind was loud and there was a faint flow of thunder along the Sound. All the lights were going on in West Egg now; the electric trains, men-carrying, were plunging home through the rain from New York. It was the hour of a profound human change, and excitement was generating on the air.

One thing's sure and nothing's surer
The rich get richer and the poor get—children.
In the meantime,
In between time—

As Nick and I went over to say goodbye, I saw that the expression of bewilderment had come back into Gatsby's face, as though a faint doubt had occurred to him as to the quality of his present happiness.

Almost five years! There must have been moments even that afternoon when Daisy tumbled short of his dreams—not through her own fault but because of the colossal vitality of his illusion. It had gone beyond her, beyond everything. He had thrown himself into it with a creative passion, adding to it all the time, decking it out with every bright feather that drifted his way. No amount of fire or freshness can challenge what a man will store up in his ghostly heart.

As I watched him, he adjusted himself a little, visibly. His hand took hold of hers and as she said something low in his ear, he turned toward her with a rush of emotion. I think that voice held him most with its fluctuating, feverish warmth because it couldn't be over-dreamed—that voice was a deathless song.

They had forgotten us, but Daisy glanced up and held out her hand; Gatsby didn't know us now at all. We looked once more at them and they looked back at us, remotely, possessed by intense life. Then Nick and I went out of the room and down the marble steps into the rain, leaving them there together.

Chapter Six

About this time an ambitious young reporter from New York arrived one morning at Gatsby's door and asked him if he had anything to say.

"Anything to say about what?" inquired Gatsby politely.

"Why—any statement to give out."

It transpired after a confused five minutes that the man had heard Gatsby's name around his office in a connection which he either wouldn't reveal or didn't fully understand. This was his day off and with laudable initiative he had hurried out "to see."

It was a random shot, and yet the reporter's instinct was right. Gatsby's notoriety, spread about by the hundreds who had accepted his hospitality and so become authorities on his past, had increased all summer until he fell just short of being news.

Contemporary legends, such as the "underground pipeline to Canada," attached themselves to him, and there was one persistent story that he didn't live in a house at all, but in a boat that looked like a house and was moved secretly up and down the Long Island shore. Just why these inventions were a source of satisfaction to James Gatz of North Dakota, isn't easy to say.

James Gatz—that was really, or at least legally, his name. He had changed it at the age of seventeen and at the specific moment that witnessed the beginning of his career—when he saw Dan Cody's yacht drop anchor over the most insidious flat on Lake Superior. It was James Gatz who had been loafing along the beach that afternoon in a torn green jersey and a pair of canvas pants, but it was already Jay Gatsby who borrowed a rowboat, pulled out to the *Tuolomee* and informed Cody that a wind might catch him and break him up in half an hour.

I suppose he'd had the name ready for a long time, even then. His parents were shiftless and unsuccessful farm people—his imagination had never really accepted them as his parents at all. The truth was that Jay Gatsby, of West Egg, Long Island, sprang from his Platonic conception of himself. He was a son of God —a phrase which, if it means anything, means just that —and he must be about His Father's Business, the service of a vast, vulgar and meretricious beauty. So he invented just the sort of Jay Gatsby that a seventeen-year-old boy would be likely to invent, and to this conception he was faithful to the end.

For over a year he had been beating his way along the south shore of Lake Superior as a clam digger and a salmon fisher or in any other capacity that brought him food and bed. His brown, hardening body lived naturally through the half fierce, half lazy work of the bracing days.

He knew women early and since they spoiled him he became contemptuous of them, of young virgins because they were ignorant, of the others because they were hysterical about things which in his overwhelming self-absorption he took for granted.

But his heart was in a constant, turbulent riot. The most grotesque and fantastic conceits haunted him in his bed at night. A universe of ineffable gaudiness spun itself out in his brain while the clock ticked on the washstand and the moon soaked with wet light his tangled clothes upon the floor. Each night he added to the pattern of his fancies until drowsiness closed down upon some vivid scene with an oblivious embrace. For a while these reveries provided an outlet for his imagination; they were a satisfactory hint of the unreality of reality, a promise that the rock of the world was founded securely on a fairy's wing.

An instinct toward his future glory had led him, some months before, to the small Lutheran college of St. Olaf in southern Minnesota. He stayed there two weeks, dismayed at its ferocious indifference to the drums of his destiny, to destiny itself, and despising the janitor's work with which he was to pay his way through. Then he drifted back to Lake Superior, and he was still searching for something to do on the day that Dan Cody's yacht dropped anchor in the shallows along shore.

Cody was fifty years old then, a product of the Nevada silver fields, of the Yukon, of every rush for metal since Seventy-five. The transactions in Montana copper that made him many times a millionaire found him physically robust but on the verge of soft-mindedness, and—suspecting this—an infinite number of women tried to separate him from his money. The none too savory ramifications by which Ella Kaye, the newspaper woman, played Madame de Maintenon to his weakness and sent him to sea in a yacht, were common knowledge to the turgid journalism of 1902. He had been coasting along all too hospitable shores for five years when he turned up as James Gatz's destiny at Little Girl Bay.

To the young Gatz, resting on his oars and looking up at the railed deck, the yacht represented all the beauty and glamor in the world. I suppose he smiled at Cody—he had probably discovered that people liked him when he smiled. At any rate, Cody asked him a few questions (one of them elicited the brand-new name) and found that he was quick, and extravagantly ambitious. A few days later he took him to Duluth and bought him a blue coat, six pair of white duck trousers and a yachting cap. And when the *Tuolomee* left for the West Indies and the Barbary Coast, Gatsby left too.

He was employed in a vague personal capacity—while he remained with Cody, he was in turn steward, mate, skipper, secretary, and even jailor. For Dan Cody sober knew what lavish doings Dan Cody drunk might soon be about, and he provided for such contingencies by reposing more and more trust in Gatsby. The arrangement lasted five years, during which the boat went three times around the continent. It might have lasted indefinitely except for the fact that Ella Kaye came on board one night in Boston and a week later Dan Cody inhospitably died.

I remember the portrait of him up in Gatsby's bedroom, a grey, florid man with a hard empty face— the pioneer debauchee who during one phase of American life brought back to the eastern seaboard the savage violence of the frontier brothel and saloon. It was indirectly due to Cody that Gatsby drank so little. Sometimes, in the course of gay parties, women used to rub champagne into his hair; for himself he formed the habit of letting liquor alone.

And it was from Cody that he inherited money—a legacy of twenty-five thousand dollars. He didn't get it. He never understood the legal device that was used against him, but what remained of the millions went intact to Ella Kaye. He was left with his singularly appropriate education; the vague contour of Jay Gatsby had filled out to the substantiality of a man.

He told all this very much later to Nick and me, but Nick put it down on paper with the idea of exploding those first wild rumors about his antecedents, which weren't even faintly true. Moreover, he told it to us at a time of confusion, when we had reached the point of believing everything and nothing about him. So let me take advantage of this short halt, while Gatsby, so to speak, caught his breath, to clear this set of misconceptions away.

It was a halt, too, in our association with his affairs. For several weeks we didn't see him or hear his voice on the phone—mostly Nick and I were in New York, trotting around with Jordan as Nick tried to ingratiate himself with her senile aunt, who took to me instantly but less so to Nick—but finally we went over to his house one Sunday afternoon.

We hadn't been there two minutes when somebody brought Tom Buchanan in for a drink. I was startled, naturally, but the really surprising thing was that it hadn't happened before.

They were a party of three on horseback—Tom and a man named Sloane and a pretty woman in a brown riding habit who had been there previously. The horses, however, were new to me; I eyed them suspiciously, as one racer measures the competition.

"I'm delighted to see you," said Gatsby standing on his porch. "I'm delighted that you dropped in."

As though they cared!

"Sit right down. Have a cigarette or a cigar." He walked around the room quickly, ringing bells. "I'll have something to drink for you in just a minute."

To me, he appeared to be profoundly affected by the fact that Tom was there. But he would be uneasy anyhow until he had given them something, realizing in a vague way that that was all they came for. Mr. Sloane wanted nothing. A lemonade? No, thanks. A little champagne? Nothing at all, thanks...I'm sorry—

"Did you have a nice ride?"

"Very good roads around here."

"I suppose the automobiles—"

"Yeah."

Moved by an irresistible impulse, Gatsby turned to Tom who had accepted the introduction as a stranger.

"I believe we've met somewhere before, Mr. Buchanan."

"Oh, yes," said Tom, gruffly polite but obviously not remembering. "So we did. I remember very well."

"About two weeks ago."

"That's right. You were with Nick here."

"I know your wife," continued Gatsby, almost aggressively.

"That so?"

Tom turned to Nick.

"You live near here, Nick?"

"Next door."

"That so?"

Mr. Sloane didn't enter into the conversation but lounged back haughtily in his chair; the woman said nothing either—until unexpectedly, after two highballs, she became cordial.

"We'll all come over to your next party, Mr. Gatsby," she suggested. "What do you say?"

"Certainly. I'd be delighted to have you."

"Be ver' nice," said Mr. Sloane, without gratitude. "Well—think we ought to be starting home."

"Please don't hurry," Gatsby urged them. He had control of himself now and he wanted to see more of Tom. "Why don't you—why don't you stay for supper? I wouldn't be surprised if some other people dropped in from New York."

"You come to supper with *me*," said the lady enthusiastically. "Both of you."

This included Nick, but I sensed she wasn't including me in her invitation. Mr. Sloane got to his feet.

"Come along," he said—but to her only.

"I mean it," she insisted. "I'd love to have you. Lots of room."

Gatsby looked at Nick questioningly. He wanted to go and he didn't see that Mr. Sloane had determined he shouldn't.

"I'm afraid I won't be able to," Nick said.

"Well, you come," she urged, concentrating on Gatsby.

Mr. Sloane murmured something close to her ear.

"We won't be late if we start now," she insisted aloud.

"I haven't got a horse," said Gatsby. "I used to ride in the army, but I've never bought a horse. I'll have to follow you in my car. Excuse me for just a minute."

The rest of us walked out on the porch, where Sloane and the lady began an impassioned conversation aside.

"My God, I believe the man's coming," said Tom. "Doesn't he know she doesn't want him?"

"She says she does want him."

"She has a big dinner party and he won't know a soul there." He frowned. "I wonder where in the devil he met Daisy. By God, I may be old-fashioned in my ideas, but women run around too much these days to suit me. They meet all kinds of crazy fish."

Suddenly Mr. Sloane and the lady walked down the steps and mounted their horses.

"Come on," said Mr. Sloane to Tom, "we're late. We've got to go." And then to Nick: "Tell him we couldn't wait, will you?"

Tom and Nick shook hands, while the others exchanged a cool nod. They trotted quickly down the drive, disappearing under the August foliage just as Gatsby, with hat and light overcoat in hand, came out the front door.

Tom was evidently perturbed at Daisy's running around alone, for on the following Saturday night he came with her to Gatsby's party. Perhaps his presence gave the evening its peculiar quality of oppressiveness —it stands out in my memory from Gatsby's other parties that summer. There were the same people, or at least the same sort of people, the same profusion of champagne, the same many-colored, many-keyed commotion, but I felt an unpleasantness in the air, a pervading harshness that hadn't been there before. Or perhaps I had merely grown used to it, grown to accept West Egg as a world complete in itself, with its own standards and its own great figures, second to nothing because it had no consciousness of being so, and now I was looking at it again, through Daisy's eyes.

It is invariably saddening to look through new eyes at things upon which you have expended your own powers of adjustment.

They arrived at twilight and as we strolled out among the sparkling hundreds, Daisy's voice was playing murmurous tricks in her throat.

"These things excite me so," she whispered to Nick, but well within my earshot. "If you want to kiss me any time during the evening, Nick, just let me know and I'll be glad to arrange it for you. Just mention my name. Or present a green card. I'm giving out green—"

"Look around," suggested Gatsby.

"I'm looking around. I'm having a marvelous—"

"You must see the faces of many people you've heard about."

Tom's arrogant eyes roamed the crowd.

"We don't go around very much," he said. "In fact, I was just thinking I don't know a soul here."

"Perhaps you know that lady." Gatsby indicated a gorgeous, scarcely human orchid of a woman who sat in state under a white plum tree. Tom and Daisy stared, with that peculiarly unreal feeling that accompanies the recognition of a hitherto ghostly celebrity of the movies.

"She's lovely," said Daisy.

"The man bending over her is her director."

He took them ceremoniously from group to group:

"Mrs. Buchanan...and Mr. Buchanan—" After an instant's hesitation he added: "the polo player."

"Oh no," objected Tom quickly. "Not me."

But evidently the sound of it pleased Gatsby, for Tom remained "the polo player" for the rest of the evening.

"I've never met so many celebrities!" Daisy exclaimed. "I liked that man—what was his name?—with the sort of blue nose."

Gatsby identified him, adding that he was a small producer.

"Well, I liked him anyhow."

"I'd a little rather not be the polo player," said Tom pleasantly. "I'd rather look at all these famous people in —in oblivion."

Daisy and Gatsby danced. I remember being surprised by his graceful, conservative fox-trot—I had never seen him dance before. Then they sauntered over to our house and sat on the steps for half an hour while, at her request, Nick and I remained watchfully in the garden: "In case there's a fire or a flood," she explained, "or any act of God."

Tom appeared from his oblivion as we were sitting down to supper together. "Do you mind if I eat with some people over here?" he said. "A fellow's getting off some funny stuff."

"Go ahead," answered Daisy genially, "And if you want to take down any addresses here's my little gold pencil..." She looked around after a moment and told

Nick the girl was "common but pretty," and I knew that except for the half hour she'd been alone with Gatsby, she wasn't having a good time.

They were at a particularly tipsy table. That was Nick's fault—Gatsby had been called to the phone and I know Nick had enjoyed these same people only two weeks before. But what had amused him then turned septic on the air now.

"How do you feel, Miss Baedeker?"

The girl addressed was trying, unsuccessfully, to slump against Nick's shoulder. At this inquiry she sat up and opened her eyes.

"Wha?"

A massive and lethargic woman, who had been urging Daisy to play golf with her at the local club tomorrow, spoke in Miss Baedeker's defense:

"Oh, she's all right now. When she's had five or six cocktails, she always starts screaming like that. I tell her she ought to leave it alone."

"I do leave it alone," affirmed the accused hollowly.

"We heard you yelling, so I said to Doc Civet here: 'There's somebody that needs your help, Doc.' "

"She's much obliged, I'm sure," said another friend, without gratitude. "But you got her dress all wet when you stuck her head in the pool."

"Anything I hate is to get my head stuck in a pool," mumbled Miss Baedeker. "They almost drowned me once over in New Jersey."

"Then you ought to leave it alone," countered Doctor Civet.

"Speak for yourself!" cried Miss Baedeker violently. "Your hand shakes. I wouldn't let you operate on me!"

It was like that. Almost the last thing I remember was standing with Nick and Daisy and watching the moving picture director and his Star. They were still under the white plum tree and their faces were touching except for a pale thin ray of moonlight between. It occurred to me that he had been very slowly bending toward her all evening to attain this proximity, and even while I watched I saw him stoop one ultimate degree and kiss at her cheek.

"I like her," said Daisy. "I think she's lovely."

But the rest offended her—and inarguably, because it wasn't a gesture but an emotion. She was appalled by West Egg, this unprecedented "place" that Broadway had begotten upon a Long Island fishing village—appalled by its raw vigor that chafed under the old euphemisms and by the too obtrusive fate that herded its inhabitants along a short cut from nothing to nothing. She saw something awful in the very simplicity she failed to understand.

Nick and I sat on the front steps with them while they waited for their car. It was dark here in front: only the bright door sent ten square feet of light volleying out into the soft black morning. Sometimes a shadow moved against a dressing-room blind above, gave way to another shadow, an indefinite procession of shadows, who rouged and powdered in an invisible glass.

"Who is this Gatsby anyhow?" demanded Tom suddenly. "Some big bootlegger?"

"Where'd you hear that?" Nick inquired.

"I didn't hear it. I imagined it. A lot of these newly rich people are just big bootleggers, you know."

"Not Gatsby," Nick said shortly.

He was silent for a moment. The pebbles of the drive crunched under his feet.

"Well, he certainly must have strained himself to get this menagerie together."

A breeze stirred the grey haze of Daisy's fur collar. I felt it tickle my ears as well.

"At least they're more interesting than the people we know," she said with an effort.

"You didn't look so interested."

"Well, I was."

Tom laughed and turned to Nick.

"Did you notice Daisy's face when that girl asked her to put her under a cold shower?"

Daisy began to sing with the music in a husky, rhythmic whisper, bringing out a meaning in each word that it had never had before and would never have again. When the melody rose, her voice broke up sweetly, following it, in a way contralto voices have. And each change tipped out a little of her warm human magic upon the air.

"Lots of people come who haven't been invited," she said suddenly. "That girl hadn't been invited. They simply force their way in and he's too polite to object."

"I'd like to know who he is and what he does," insisted Tom. "And I think I'll make a point of finding out."

"I can tell you right now," she answered. "He

owned some drug stores, a lot of drug stores. He built them up himself."

The dilatory limousine came rolling up the drive.

"Good night, Nick, good night, Dash," said Daisy, giving my head a quick but loving pat.

Her glance left me and sought the lighted top of the steps where "Three O'Clock in the Morning," a neat, sad little waltz of that year, was drifting out the open door.

After all, in the very casualness of Gatsby's party, there were romantic possibilities totally absent from her world. What was it up there in the song that seemed to be calling her back inside? What would happen now in the dim incalculable hours? Perhaps some unbelievable guest would arrive, a person infinitely rare and to be marveled at, some authentically radiant young girl who with one fresh glance at Gatsby, one moment of magical encounter, would blot out those five years of unwavering devotion.

We stayed late that night. Gatsby asked us to wait until he was free and we lingered in the garden until the inevitable swimming party had run up, chilled and exalted, from the black beach, until the lights were extinguished in the guest rooms overhead. When he came down the steps at last, the tanned skin was drawn unusually tight on his face, and his eyes were bright and tired.

"She didn't like it," he said immediately.

"Of course she did."

"She didn't like it," he insisted. "She didn't have a good time."

He was silent and I guessed at his unutterable depression.

"I feel far away from her," he said. "It's hard to make her understand."

"You mean about the dance?"

"The dance?" He dismissed all the dances he had given with a snap of his fingers. "Old sport, the dance is unimportant."

He wanted nothing less of Daisy than that she should go to Tom and say: "I never loved you." After she had obliterated three years with that sentence, they could decide upon the more practical measures to be taken. One of them was that, after she was free, they were to go back to Louisville and be married from her house—just as if it were five years ago.

"And she doesn't understand," he said. "She used to be able to understand. We'd sit for hours—"

He broke off and began to walk up and down a desolate path of fruit rinds and discarded favors and crushed flowers.

"I wouldn't ask too much of her," Nick ventured. "You can't repeat the past."

"Can't repeat the past?" he cried incredulously. "Why of course you can!"

He looked around him wildly, as if the past were lurking here in the shadow of his house, just out of reach of his hand.

"I'm going to fix everything just the way it was before," he said, nodding determinedly. "She'll see."

He talked a lot about the past and I gathered that he wanted to recover something, some idea of himself perhaps, that had gone into loving Daisy. His life had been confused and disordered since then, but if he could once return to a certain starting place and go over it all slowly, he could find out what that thing was...

...One autumn night, five years before, they had been walking down the street when the leaves were falling, and they came to a place where there were no trees and the sidewalk was white with moonlight. They stopped here and turned toward each other. Now it was a cool night with that mysterious excitement in it which comes at the two changes of the year. The quiet lights in the houses were humming out into the darkness and there was a stir and bustle among the stars. Out of the corner of his eye, Gatsby saw that the blocks of the sidewalk really formed a ladder and mounted to a secret place above the trees—he could climb to it, if he climbed alone, and once there he could suck on the pap of life, gulp down the incomparable milk of wonder.

His heartbeat faster and faster as Daisy's white face came up to his own. He knew that when he kissed this girl, and forever wed his unutterable visions to her perishable breath, his mind would never romp again like the mind of God. So he waited, listening for a moment longer to the tuning fork that had been struck upon a star. Then he kissed her. At his lips' touch, she blossomed for him like a flower and the incarnation was complete.

Through all he said, even through his appalling sentimentality, I was reminded of something—an elusive rhythm, a fragment of lost words, that I had heard somewhere a long time ago.

But they made no sound and what I had almost remembered was uncommunicable forever.

____

Chapter Seven

I t was when curiosity about Gatsby was at its highest that the lights in his house failed to go on one Saturday night—and, as obscurely as it had begun, his career as Trimalchio was over.

Only gradually did I become aware that the automobiles which turned expectantly into his drive stayed for just a minute and then drove sulkily away. Wondering if he were sick, Nick and I went over to find out—an unfamiliar butler with a villainous face squinted at us suspiciously from the door.

"Is Mr. Gatsby sick?"

"Nope." After a pause he added "sir" in a dilatory, grudging way.

"I hadn't seen him around, and I was rather worried. Tell him Dash and Mr. Carraway came over."

"Who?" he demanded rudely.

"Carraway. And Dash," Nick added, glancing significantly in my direction.

"Carraway. And a dog. Dash. All right, I'll tell him." Abruptly, he slammed the door.

Our Finn informed us that Gatsby had dismissed every servant in his house a week ago and replaced them with half a dozen others, who never went into West Egg Village to be bribed by the tradesmen, but ordered moderate supplies over the telephone. The grocery boy reported that the kitchen looked like a pigsty, and the general opinion in the village was that the new people weren't servants at all.

Next day Gatsby called me on the phone.

"Going away?" Nick inquired.

"No, old sport."

"I hear you fired all your servants."

"I wanted somebody who wouldn't gossip. Daisy comes over quite often—in the afternoons."

So, the whole caravansary had fallen in like a card house at the disapproval in her eyes.

"They're some people Wolfsheim wanted to do something for. They're all brothers and sisters. They used to run a small hotel."

"I see."

He was calling up at Daisy's request—would Nick and I come to lunch at her house tomorrow? Miss Baker would be there. Half an hour later, Daisy herself telephoned and seemed relieved to find that we were coming. Something was up. And yet I couldn't believe that they would choose this occasion for a scene—especially for the rather harrowing scene that Gatsby had outlined in the garden.

The next day was broiling, almost the last, certainly

the warmest, of the summer. As our train emerged from the tunnel into sunlight, only the hot whistles of the National Biscuit Company broke the simmering hush at noon. The straw seats of the car hovered on the edge of combustion; the woman next to us perspired delicately for a while into her white shirt-waist, and then, as her newspaper dampened under her fingers, lapsed despairingly into deep heat with a desolate cry. Her pocketbook slapped to the floor next to my warm, sleeping head.

"Oh, my!" she gasped.

Nick picked it up with a weary bend and handed it back to her, holding it at arm's length and by the extreme tip of the corners to indicate that he had no designs upon it—but everyone nearby, including the woman, suspected him just the same.

Through the hall of the Buchanans' house blew a faint wind, carrying the sound of the telephone bell out to Gatsby and us as we waited at the door.

"The master's body!" roared the butler into the mouthpiece. "I'm sorry, madame, but we can't furnish it—it's far too hot to touch this noon!"

What he really said was: "Yes...yes...I'll see."

He set down the receiver and came toward us, glistening slightly, to take our stiff straw hats.

"Madame expects you in the salon!" he cried, needlessly indicating the direction. In this heat every extra gesture was an affront to the common store of life.

The room, shadowed well with awnings, was dark and cool. Daisy and Jordan lay upon an enormous couch, like silver idols, weighing down their own white dresses against the singing breeze of the fans.

"We can't move," they said together.

Jordan's fingers, powdered white over their tan, rested for a moment in Nick's.

"And Mr. Thomas Buchanan, the athlete?" Nick inquired.

Simultaneously I heard his voice, gruff, muffled, husky, at the hall telephone.

Gatsby stood in the center of the crimson carpet and gazed around with fascinated eyes. Daisy watched him and laughed, her sweet, exciting laugh; a tiny gust of powder rose from her bosom into the air.

"The rumor is," whispered Jordan, "that that's Tom's girl on the telephone."

We were silent. The voice in the hall rose high with annoyance. "Very well, then, I won't sell you the car at all...I'm under no obligations to you at all...And as for your bothering me about it at lunch time I won't stand that at all!"

"Holding down the receiver," said Daisy cynically.

"No, he's not," Nick assured her. "It's a bona fide deal. I happen to know about it."

Tom flung open the door, blocked out its space for a moment with his thick body, and hurried into the room.

"Mr. Gatsby!" He put out his broad, flat hand with well-concealed dislike. "I'm glad to see you, sir...Nick... and, of course, the faithful Dash..."

"Make us a cold drink," cried Daisy.

As he left the room again, she got up and went over to Gatsby and pulled his face down kissing him on the mouth.

"You know I love you," she murmured.

"You forget there's a lady present," said Jordan.

Daisy looked around doubtfully.

"You kiss Nick too."

"What a low, vulgar girl!"

"I don't care!" cried Daisy and began to clog on the brick fireplace. Then she remembered the heat and sat down guiltily on the couch just as a freshly laundered nurse leading a little girl came into the room.

"Bles-sed pre-cious," she crooned, holding out her arms. "Come to your own mother that loves you."

The child, relinquished by the nurse, rushed across the room and rooted shyly into her mother's dress.

"The Bles-sed pre-cious! Did mother get powder on your old yellowy hair? Stand up now and say How-de-do."

Gatsby and Nick in turn leaned down and took the small reluctant hand. Afterward he kept looking at the child with surprise. I don't think he had ever really believed in its existence before.

"I got dressed before luncheon," said the child, turning cageily to Daisy.

"That's because your mother wanted to show you off." Her face bent into the single wrinkle of the small white neck. "You dream, you. You absolute little dream."

"Yes," admitted the child calmly. "Aunt Jordan's got on a white dress too."

"How do you like mother's friends?" Daisy turned her around so that she faced Gatsby. "Do you think they're pretty? Isn't that a pretty dog?"

"Where's Daddy?" The child expressed no interest in any of us, not even me.

"She doesn't look like her father," explained Daisy. "She looks like me. She's got my hair and shape of the face."

Daisy sat back upon the couch. The nurse took a step forward and held out her hand.

"Come, Pammy."

"Goodbye, sweetheart!"

With a reluctant backward glance, the well-disciplined child held to her nurse's hand and was pulled out the door, just as Tom came back, preceding four gin rickeys that clicked full of ice.

Gatsby took up his drink.

"They certainly look cool," he said, with visible tension.

They drank in long greedy swallows. The staff had kindly left a bowl of water on the floor for me. I sipped at it my drink more daintily than the humans.

"I read somewhere that the sun's getting hotter every year," said Tom genially. "It seems that pretty soon the earth's going to fall into the sun—or wait a minute—it's just the opposite—the sun's getting colder every year. Come outside," he suggested to Gatsby. "I'd like you to have a look at the place."

Nick and I went with them out to the veranda. On

the green Sound, stagnant in the heat, one small sail crawled slowly toward the fresher sea. Gatsby's eyes followed it momentarily; he raised his hand and pointed across the bay.

"I'm right across from you."

"So you are."

Our eyes lifted over the rosebeds and the hot lawn and the weedy refuse of the dog days along shore—dog days, a term which still left me baffled. Slowly the white wings of the boat moved against the blue cool limit of the sky. Ahead lay the scalloped ocean and the abounding blessed isles.

"There's sport for you," said Tom, nodding. "I'd like to be out there with him for about an hour."

We had luncheon in the dining-room, darkened, too, against the heat, and the humans drank down nervous gayety with the cold ale. I supped happily on some dry kibble, which Nick had secreted with him from home.

"What'll we do with ourselves this afternoon," cried Daisy. "And the day after that, and the next thirty years?"

"Don't be morbid," Jordan said. "Life starts all over again when it gets crisp in the fall."

"But it's so hot," insisted Daisy, on the verge of tears. "And everything's so confused. Let's all go to town!"

Her voice struggled on through the heat, beating against it, molding its senselessness into forms.

"I've heard of making a garage out of a stable," Tom was saying to Gatsby. "But I'm the first man who ever made a stable out of a garage."

"Who wants to go to town?" demanded Daisy insistently. Gatsby's eyes floated toward her. "Ah," she cried, "you look so cool."

Their eyes met, and they stared together at each other, alone in space. With an effort she glanced down at the table.

"You always look so cool," she repeated.

She had told him that she loved him, and Tom Buchanan saw. He was astounded. His mouth opened a little and he looked at Gatsby and then back at Daisy as if he had just recognized her as someone he knew a long time ago.

"You resemble the advertisement of the man," she went on innocently. "You know the advertisement of the man——"

"All right," broke in Tom quickly. "I'm perfectly willing to go to town. Come on——we're all going to town."

He got up, his eyes still flashing between Gatsby and his wife. No one moved.

"Come on!" His temper cracked a little. "What's the matter, anyhow? If we're going to town let's start."

His hand, trembling with his effort at self-control, bore to his lips the last of his glass of ale. Daisy's voice got us to our feet and out on to the blazing gravel drive.

"Are we just going to go?" she objected. "Like this? Aren't we going to let anyone smoke a cigarette first?"

"Everybody smoked all through lunch."

"Oh, let's have fun," she begged him. "It's too hot to fuss."

He didn't answer.

"Have it your own way," she said. "Come on, Jordan."

They went upstairs to get ready while the three men and the one dog stood there shuffling the hot pebbles with our feet. A silver curve of the moon hovered already in the western sky. Gatsby started to speak, changed his mind, but not before Tom wheeled and faced him expectantly.

"Have you got your stables here?" asked Gatsby with an effort.

"About a quarter of a mile down the road."

"Oh."

A pause.

"I don't see the idea of going to town," broke out Tom savagely. "Women get these notions in their heads—"

"Shall we take anything to drink?" called Daisy from an upper window.

"I'll get some whiskey," answered Tom. He went inside.

Gatsby turned to Nick rigidly:

"I can't say anything in his house, old sport."

"She's got an indiscreet voice," Nick remarked. "It's full of—"

Nick hesitated.

"Her voice is full of money," Gatsby said suddenly.

That was it. I'd never understood before. It was full of money—that was the inexhaustible charm that rose and fell in it, the jingle of it, the cymbals' song of it...High in a white palace the king's daughter, the golden girl...

Tom came out of the house wrapping a quart bottle in a towel, followed by Daisy and Jordan wearing small tight hats of metallic cloth and carrying light capes over their arms.

"Shall we all go in my car?" suggested Gatsby. He felt the hot, green leather of the seat. "I ought to have left it in the shade."

"Is it standard shift?" demanded Tom.

"Yes."

"Well, you take my coupé and let me drive your car to town."

The suggestion was distasteful to Gatsby.

"I don't think there's much gas," he objected.

"Plenty of gas," said Tom boisterously. He looked at the gauge. "And if it runs out, I can stop at a drug store. You can buy anything at a drug store nowadays."

A pause followed this apparently pointless remark. Daisy looked at Tom frowning and an indefinable expression, at once definitely unfamiliar and vaguely recognizable, as if I had only heard it described in words, passed over Gatsby's face.

"Come on, Daisy," said Tom, pressing her with his hand toward Gatsby's car. "I'll take you in this circus wagon."

He opened the door, but she moved out from the circle of his arm.

"You take Nick and Jordan and Dash. We'll follow you in the coupé."

She walked close to Gatsby, touching his coat with her hand. Jordan and Tom and Nick and I got into Gatsby's car, Tom pushed the unfamiliar gears tentatively, and we shot off into the oppressive heat leaving them out of sight behind.

"Did you see that?" demanded Tom.

"See what?"

He looked at Nick keenly, realizing that he and Jordan must have known all along.

"You think I'm pretty dumb, don't you?" he suggested. "Perhaps I am, but I have a—almost a second sight, sometimes, that tells me what to do. Maybe you don't believe that, but science—"

He paused. The immediate contingency overtook him, pulled him back from the edge of the theoretical abyss.

"I've made a small investigation of this fellow," he continued. "I could have gone deeper if I'd known—"

"Do you mean you've been to a medium?" inquired Jordan humorously.

"What?" Confused, he stared at them as they laughed. "A medium?"

"About Gatsby."

"About Gatsby! No, I haven't. I said I'd been making a small investigation of his past."

"And you found he was an Oxford man," said Jordan helpfully.

"An Oxford man!" He was incredulous. "Like hell he is! He wears a pink suit."

"Nevertheless, he's an Oxford man."

"Oxford, New Mexico," snorted Tom contemptuously. "Or something like that."

"Listen, Tom. If you're such a snob, why did you invite him to lunch?" demanded Jordan crossly.

"Daisy invited him; she knew him before we were married—God knows where!"

They were all irritable now with the fading ale and, aware of it. We drove for a while in silence. Then as Doctor T. J. Eckleburg's faded eyes came into sight down the road, I remembered Gatsby's caution about gasoline.

"We've got enough to get us to town," said Tom.

"But there's a garage right here," objected Jordan. "I don't want to get stalled in this baking heat."

Tom threw on both brakes impatiently and we slid to an abrupt dusty stop under Wilson's sign. After a moment the proprietor emerged from the interior of his establishment and gazed hollow-eyed at the car.

"Let's have some gas!" cried Tom roughly. "What do you think we stopped for—to admire the view?"

"I'm sick," said Wilson without moving. "I been sick all day."

"What's the matter?"

"I'm all run down."

"Well, shall I help myself?" Tom demanded. "You sounded well enough on the phone."

With an effort Wilson left the shade and support of the doorway and, breathing hard, unscrewed the cap of the tank. In the sunlight his face was green.

"I didn't mean to interrupt your lunch," he said.

"But I need money pretty bad and I was wondering what you were going to do with your old car."

"How do you like this one?" inquired Tom. "I bought it last week."

"It's a nice yellow one," said Wilson, as he strained at the handle.

"Like to buy it?"

"Big chance," Wilson smiled faintly. "No, but I could make some money on the other."

"What do you want money for, all of a sudden?"

"I've been here too long. I want to get away. My wife and I want to go west."

"Your wife does!" exclaimed Tom, startled.

"She's been talking about it for ten years." He rested for a moment against the pump, shading his eyes. "And now she's going whether she wants to or not. I'm going to get her away."

The coupé flashed by us with a flurry of dust and the flash of a waving hand.

"What do I owe you?" demanded Tom harshly.

"I just got wised up to something funny the last two days," remarked Wilson. "That's why I want to get away. That's why I been bothering you about the car."

"What do I owe you?"

"Dollar twenty."

The relentless beating heat was beginning to confuse me, and I had a bad moment there before I realized that so far his suspicions hadn't alighted on Tom. He had discovered that Myrtle had some sort of life apart from him in another world, and the shock had made him physically sick.

I stared at him and then at Tom, who had made a parallel discovery less than an hour before—and it occurred to me that there was no difference between men, in intelligence or race, so profound as the difference between the sick and the well. Wilson was so sick that he looked guilty, unforgivably guilty—as if he had just got some poor girl with child.

"I'll let you have that car," said Tom. "I'll send it over tomorrow afternoon."

That locality was always vaguely disquieting, even in the broad glare of afternoon, and now I turned my head as though I had been warned of something behind. Over the ash heaps the giant eyes of Doctor T. J. Eckleburg kept their vigil, but I perceived, after a moment, that other eyes were regarding us with peculiar intensity from less than twenty feet away.

In one of the windows over the garage, the curtains had been moved aside a little and Myrtle Wilson was peering down at the car. So engrossed was she that she had no consciousness of being observed, and one emotion after another crept into her face like objects into a slowly developing picture.

Her expression was curiously familiar—it was an expression I had often seen on women's faces. But on Myrtle Wilson's face, it seemed purposeless and inexplicable, until I realized that her eyes, wide with jealous terror, were fixed not on Tom, but on Jordan Baker, whom she took to be his wife.

~

There is no confusion like the confusion of a simple mind, and as we drove away I could tell Tom was feeling the hot whips of panic. His wife and his mistress, until an hour ago secure and inviolate, were slipping precipitately from his control. Instinct made him step on the accelerator with the double purpose of overtaking Daisy and leaving Wilson behind. We sped along toward Astoria at fifty miles an hour, until, among the spidery girders of the elevated, we came in sight of the easygoing blue coupé.

"Those big movies around Fiftieth Street are cool," suggested Jordan. "I love New York on summer after-noons when every one's away. There's something very sensuous about it—overripe, as if all sorts of funny fruits were going to fall into your hands."

I sensed the word "sensuous" had the effect of further disquieting Tom, but before he could invent a protest, the coupé came to a stop and Daisy signaled us to draw up alongside.

"Where are we going?" she cried.

"How about the movies?"

"It's so hot," she complained. "You go. We'll ride around and meet you after." With an effort her wit rose faintly. "We'll meet you on some corner. I'll be the man smoking two cigarettes."

"We can't argue about it here," Tom said impa-tiently as a truck gave out a cursing whistle behind us. "You follow me to the south side of Central Park, in front of the Plaza."

Several times he turned his head and looked back for their car, and if the traffic delayed them, he slowed up until they came into sight. I think he was afraid they would dart down a side street and out of his life forever.

But they didn't. And we all took the less explicable step of engaging the parlor of a suite in the Plaza Hotel.

The prolonged and tumultuous argument that ended by herding us into that room eludes me, though I have a sharp physical memory the human voices, so sharp, like the pained yelps of unhappy pups. The notion originated with Daisy's suggestion that we hire five bathrooms and take cold baths, and then assumed more tangible form as "a place to have a mint julep." Each of the humans said over and over that it was a "crazy idea"—they all talked at once to a baffled clerk and thought, or pretended to think, that they were being very funny...

The room was large and stifling, and, though it was already four o'clock, opening the windows admitted only a gust of hot shrubbery from the Park. Daisy went to the mirror and stood with her back to us, fixing her hair.

"It's a swell suite," whispered Jordan respectfully and everyone laughed.

"Open another window," commanded Daisy, without turning around.

"There aren't any more."

"Well, we'd better telephone for an axe—"

"The thing to do is to forget about the heat," said Tom impatiently. "You make it ten times worse by crabbing about it."

He unrolled the bottle of whiskey from the towel and put it on the table.

"Why not let her alone, old sport?" remarked Gatsby.

"You're the one that wanted to come to town."

There was a moment of silence. The telephone book slipped from its nail and splashed to the floor, whereupon Jordan whispered "Excuse me"—but this time no one laughed.

"I'll pick it up," Nick offered.

"I've got it." Gatsby examined the parted string, muttered "Hum!" in an interested way, and tossed the book on a chair.

"That's a great expression of yours, isn't it?" said Tom sharply.

"What is?"

"All this 'old sport' business. Where'd you pick that up?"

"Now see here, Tom," said Daisy, turning around from the mirror. "If you're going to make personal remarks, I won't stay here a minute. Call up and order some ice for the mint julep."

As Tom took up the receiver, the compressed heat exploded into sound and we were listening to the portentous chords of Mendelssohn's Wedding March from the ballroom below.

"Imagine marrying anybody in this heat!" cried Jordan dismally.

"Still—I was married in the middle of June," Daisy remembered. "Louisville in June! Somebody fainted. Who was it fainted, Tom?"

"Biloxi," he answered shortly.

"A man named Biloxi. 'Blocks' Biloxi, and he made boxes—that's a fact—and he was from Biloxi, Tennessee."

"They carried him into my house," appended Jordan. "Because we lived just two doors from the church. And he stayed three weeks, until Daddy told him he had to get out. The day after he left, Daddy died." After a moment she added as if she might have sounded irreverent, "There wasn't any connection."

"I used to know a Bill Biloxi from Memphis," Nick remarked.

"That was his cousin. I knew his whole family history before he left. He gave me an aluminum putter that I use today."

The music had died down as the ceremony began and now a long cheer floated in at the window, followed by intermittent cries of "Yea—ea—ea!" and finally by a burst of jazz as the dancing began.

"We're getting old," said Daisy. "If we were young, we'd rise and dance."

"Remember Biloxi," Jordan warned her. "Where'd you know him, Tom?"

"Biloxi?" He concentrated with an effort. "I didn't know him. He was a friend of Daisy's."

"He was not," she denied. "I'd never seen him before. He came down in the private car."

"Well, he said he knew you. He said he was raised in Louisville. Asa Bird brought him around at the last minute and asked if we had room for him."

Jordan smiled. "He was probably bumming his way

home. He told me he was president of your class at Yale."

Tom and Nick looked at each other blankly.

"Biloxi?"

"First place, we didn't have any president—"

Gatsby's foot beat a short, restless tattoo and Tom eyed him suddenly.

"By the way, Mr. Gatsby, I understand you're an Oxford man."

"Not exactly."

"Oh, yes, I understand you went to Oxford."

"Yes—I went there."

A pause. Then Tom's voice, incredulous and insulting:

"You must have gone there about the time Biloxi went to New Haven."

Another pause. A waiter knocked and came in with crushed mint and ice, but the silence was unbroken by his "Thank you" and the soft closing of the door. This tremendous detail was to be cleared up at last.

"I told you I went there," said Gatsby.

"I heard you, but I'd like to know when."

"It was in nineteen-nineteen, I only stayed five months. That's why I can't really call myself an Oxford man."

Tom glanced around to see if we mirrored his unbelief. But we were all looking at Gatsby.

"It was an opportunity they gave to some of the officers after the Armistice," he continued. "We could go to any of the universities in England or France."

I think Nick wanted to get up and slap him on the

back. He'd had one of those renewals of complete faith in him.

Daisy rose, smiling faintly, and went to the table.

"Open the whiskey, Tom," she ordered. "And I'll make you a mint julep. Then you won't seem so stupid to yourself...Look at the mint!"

"Wait a minute," snapped Tom. "I want to ask Mr. Gatsby one more question."

"Go on," Gatsby said politely.

"What kind of a row are you trying to cause in my house anyhow?"

They were out in the open at last and Gatsby was content.

"He isn't causing a row." Daisy looked desperately from one to the other. "You're causing a row. Please have a little self-control."

"Self-control!" repeated Tom incredulously. "I suppose the latest thing is to sit back and let Mr. Nobody from Nowhere make love to your wife. Well, if that's the idea, you can count me out ... Nowadays people begin by sneering at family life and family institutions, and next they'll throw everything overboard and have intermarriage between black and white."

Flushed with his impassioned gibberish, he saw himself standing alone on the last barrier of civilization.

"We're all white here," murmured Jordan.

"I know I'm not very popular. I don't give big parties. I suppose you've got to make your house into a pigsty in order to have any friends—in the modern world."

Angry as Nick was, as they all were, he seemed tempted to laugh whenever Tom opened his mouth. The transition from libertine to prig was so complete.

"I've got something to tell *you*, old sport,—" began Gatsby. But Daisy guessed at his intention.

"Please don't!" she interrupted helplessly. "Please let's all go home. Why don't we all go home?"

"That's a good idea." Nick got up, waving to me to stand. "Come on, Tom. Nobody wants a drink."

"I want to know what Mr. Gatsby has to tell me."

"Your wife doesn't love you," said Gatsby. "She's never loved you. She loves me."

"You must be crazy!" exclaimed Tom automatically.

Gatsby sprang to his feet, vivid with excitement.

"She never loved you, do you hear?" he cried. "She only married you because I was poor and she was tired of waiting for me. It was a terrible mistake, but in her heart she never loved anyone except me!"

At this point Jordan and Nick tried to go, but Tom and Gatsby insisted with competitive firmness that we remain—as though neither of them had anything to conceal and it would be a privilege to partake vicariously of their emotions.

"Sit down Daisy." Tom's voice groped unsuccessfully for the paternal note. "What's been going on? I want to hear all about it."

"I told you what's been going on," said Gatsby. "Going on for five years—and you didn't know."

Tom turned to Daisy sharply.

"You've been seeing this fellow for five years?"

"Not seeing," said Gatsby. "No, we couldn't meet. But both of us loved each other all that time, old sport, and you didn't know. I used to laugh sometimes—"

But there was no laughter in his eyes that I could see.

"—I used to laugh to think that you didn't know."

"Oh—that's all." Tom tapped his thick fingers together like a clergyman and leaned back in his chair. "You're crazy!" he exploded. "I can't speak about what happened five years ago, because I didn't know Daisy then—and I'll be damned if I see how you got within a mile of her, unless you brought the groceries to the back door. But all the rest of that's a God Damned lie. Daisy loved me when she married me, and she loves me now."

"No," said Gatsby, shaking his head.

"She does, though. The trouble is that sometimes she gets foolish ideas in her head and doesn't know what she's doing." He nodded sagely. "And what's more, I love Daisy too. Once in a while I go off on a spree and make a fool of myself, but I always come back, and in my heart I love her all the time."

"You're revolting," said Daisy. She turned to Nick, and her voice, dropping an octave lower, filled the room with thrilling scorn: "Do you know why we left Chicago? I'm surprised that they didn't treat you to the story of that little spree."

Gatsby walked over and stood beside her.

"Daisy, that's all over now," he said earnestly. "It doesn't matter anymore. Just tell him the truth—that you never loved him—and it's all wiped out forever."

She looked at him blindly. "Why—how could I love him—possibly?"

"You never loved him."

She hesitated. Her eyes fell on Jordan and Nick with a sort of appeal, as though she realized at last what she was doing—and as though she had never, all along, intended doing anything at all. But it was done now. It was too late.

"I never loved him," she said, with perceptible reluctance.

"Not at Kapiolani?" demanded Tom suddenly.

"No."

From the ballroom beneath, muffled and suffocating chords were drifting up on hot waves of air.

"Not that day I carried you down from the Punch Bowl to keep your shoes dry?" There was a husky tenderness in his tone. "...Daisy?"

"Please don't." Her voice was cold, but the rancor was gone from it. She looked at Gatsby. "There, Jay," she said—but her hand as she tried to light a cigarette was trembling. Suddenly she threw the cigarette and the burning match on the carpet.

"Oh, you want too much!" she cried to Gatsby. "I love you now—isn't that enough? I can't help what's past." She began to sob helplessly. "I did love him once—but I loved you too."

Gatsby's eyes opened and closed.

"You loved me *too*?" he repeated.

"Even that's a lie," said Tom savagely. "She didn't know you were alive. Why—there're things between

Daisy and me that you'll never know, things that neither of us can ever forget."

The words seemed to bite physically into Gatsby.

"I want to speak to Daisy alone," he insisted. "She's all excited now—"

"Even alone I can't say I never loved Tom," she admitted in a pitiful voice. "It wouldn't be true."

"Of course it wouldn't," agreed Tom.

She turned to her husband. "As if it mattered to you," she said.

"Of course it matters. I'm going to take better care of you from now on."

"You don't understand," said Gatsby, with a touch of panic. "You're not going to take care of her anymore."

"I'm not?" Tom opened his eyes wide and laughed. He could afford to control himself now. "Why's that?"

"Daisy's leaving you."

"Nonsense."

"I am, though," she said with a visible effort.

"She's not leaving me!" Tom's words suddenly leaned down over Gatsby. "Certainly not for a common swindler who'd have to steal the ring he put on her finger."

"I won't stand this!" cried Daisy. "Oh, please let's get out."

"Who are you, anyhow?" broke out Tom. "You're one of that bunch that hangs around with Meyer Wolfsheim—that much I happen to know. I've made a little investigation into your affairs—and I'll carry it further tomorrow."

"You can suit yourself about that, old sport," said Gatsby steadily.

"I found out what your 'drug stores' were." He turned to us and spoke rapidly. "He and this Wolfsheim bought up a lot of side-street drug stores here and in Chicago and sold grain alcohol over the counter. That's one of his little stunts. I picked him for a bootlegger the first time I saw him and I wasn't far wrong."

"What about it?" said Gatsby politely. "I guess your friend Walter Chase wasn't too proud to come in on it."

"And you left him in the lurch, didn't you? You let him go to jail for a month over in New Jersey. God! You ought to hear Walter on the subject of _you_."

"He came to us dead broke. He was very glad to pick up some money, old sport."

"Don't you call me 'old sport'!" cried Tom. Gatsby said nothing. "Walter could have you up on the betting laws too, but Wolfsheim scared him into shutting his mouth."

That unfamiliar yet recognizable look was back again in Gatsby's face.

"That drug store business was just small change," continued Tom slowly. "But you've got something on now that Walter's afraid to tell me about."

I glanced at Daisy who was staring terrified between Gatsby and her husband and at Jordan who had begun to balance an invisible but absorbing object on the tip of her chin and at Nick who stood frozen watching the tableau before us.

Then I turned back to Gatsby and was startled at

his expression. He looked—and this is said in all contempt for the babbled slander of his garden—as if he had "killed a man." For a moment, the set of his face could be described in just that fantastic way.

It passed, and he began to talk excitedly to Daisy, denying everything, defending his name against accusations that had not been made. But with every word, she was drawing further and further into herself. So he gave that up and only the dead dream fought on as the afternoon slipped away, trying to touch what was no longer tangible, struggling unhappily, undespairingly, toward that lost voice across the room.

The voice begged again to go.

"*Please*, Tom! I can't stand this anymore."

Her frightened eyes told that whatever intentions, whatever courage she had had, were definitely gone.

"You two start on home, Daisy," said Tom. "In Mr. Gatsby's car."

She looked at Tom, alarmed now, but he insisted with magnanimous scorn.

"Go on. He won't annoy you. I think he realizes that his presumptuous little flirtation is over."

They were gone, without a word, snapped out, made accidental, isolated, like ghosts even from our pity.

After a moment Tom got up and began wrapping the unopened bottle of whiskey in the towel.

"Want any of this stuff? Jordan? Nick?"

Nick didn't answer.

"Nick?" He asked again.

"What?"

"Want any?"

"No... I just remembered that today's my birthday."

He was thirty. Before him stretched the portentous menacing road of a new decade.

It was seven o'clock when we got into the coupé with him and started for Long Island. Tom talked incessantly, exulting and laughing, but his voice was as remote from Jordan and Nick and me as the foreign clamor on the sidewalk or the tumult of the elevated overhead.

Human sympathy—unlike canine sympathy—has its limits, and they were content to let all their tragic arguments fade with the city lights behind.

So we drove on toward death through the cooling twilight.

The young Greek, Michaelis, who ran the coffee joint beside the ash heaps was the principal witness at the inquest. He had slept through the heat until after five, when he strolled over to the garage and found George Wilson sick in his office—really sick, pale as his own pale hair and shaking all over.

Michaelis advised him to go to bed, but Wilson refused, saying that he'd miss a lot of business if he did. While his neighbor was trying to persuade him, a violent racket broke out overhead.

"I've got my wife locked in up there," explained Wilson calmly. "She's going to stay there till the day after tomorrow and then we're going to move away."

Michaelis was astonished; they had been neighbors for four years and Wilson had never seemed faintly capable of such a statement. Generally, he was one of these worn-out men: when he wasn't working, he sat on a chair in the doorway and stared at the people and the cars that passed along the road. When anyone spoke to him, he invariably laughed in an agreeable, colorless way. He was his wife's man and not his own.

So naturally Michaelis tried to find out what had happened, but Wilson wouldn't say a word—instead he began to throw curious, suspicious glances at his visitor and ask him what he'd been doing at certain times on certain days. Just as the latter was getting uneasy, some workmen came past the door bound for his restaurant and Michaelis took the opportunity to get away, intending to come back later. But he didn't. He supposed he forgot to, that's all.

When he came outside again, a little after seven, he was reminded of the conversation because he heard Mrs. Wilson's voice, loud and scolding, downstairs in the garage.

"Beat me!" he heard her cry. "Throw me down and beat me, you dirty little coward!"

A moment later she rushed out into the dusk, waving her hands and shouting; before he could move from his door the business was over.

The "death car," as the newspapers called it, didn't stop; it came out of the gathering darkness, wavered tragically for a moment, and then disappeared around the next bend.

Michaelis wasn't even sure of its color—he told the

first policeman that it was light green. The other car, the one going toward New York, came to rest a hundred yards beyond, and its driver hurried back to where Myrtle Wilson, her life violently extinguished, knelt in the road and mingled her thick, dark blood with the dust.

Michaelis and this man reached her first, but when they had torn open her shirtwaist, still damp with perspiration, they saw that her left breast was swinging loose like a flap and there was no need to listen for the heart beneath. The mouth was wide open and ripped at the corners as though she had choked a little in giving up the tremendous vitality she had stored so long.

We saw the three or four automobiles and the crowd when we were still some distance away.

"Wreck!" said Tom. "That's good. Wilson will have a little business at last."

He slowed down, but still without any intention of stopping until, as we came nearer, the hushed intent faces of the people at the garage door made him automatically put on the brakes.

"We'll take a look," he said doubtfully. "Just a look."

I became aware now of a hollow, wailing sound which issued incessantly from the garage, a sound which as we got out of the coupé and walked toward the door resolved itself into the words "Oh, my God!" uttered over and over in a gasping moan.

"There's some bad trouble here," said Tom excitedly.

He reached up on tiptoes and peered over a circle of heads into the garage which was lit only by a yellow light in a swinging wire basket overhead. Then he made a harsh sound in his throat and, with a violent thrusting movement of his powerful arms, pushed his way through.

The circle closed up again with a running murmur of expostulation; it was a minute before I could see anything at all. Then new arrivals disarranged the line and Jordan and Nick and I were pushed suddenly inside.

Myrtle Wilson's body—wrapped in a blanket and then in another blanket, as though she suffered from a chill in the hot night—lay on a worktable by the wall and Tom, with his back to us, was bending over it, motionless. Next to him stood a motorcycle policeman taking down names with much sweat and correction in a little book.

At first, I couldn't find the source of the high, groaning words that echoed clamorously through the bare garage —then I saw Wilson standing on the raised threshold of his office, swaying back and forth and holding to the doorposts with both hands. Some man was talking to him in a low voice and attempting from time to time to lay a hand on his shoulder, but Wilson neither heard nor saw. His eyes would drop slowly from the swinging light to the laden table by the wall and then jerk back to the light again and he gave out incessantly his high horrible call.

"O, my Ga-od! O, my Ga-od! Oh, Ga-od! Oh, my Ga-od!"

Presently, Tom lifted his head with a jerk and—after staring around the garage with glazed eyes—addressed a mumbled incoherent remark to the policeman.

"M-a-v—" the policeman was saying. "—o—"

"No—r—" corrected the man, "M-a-v-r-o—"

"Listen to me!" muttered Tom fiercely.

"r—" said the policeman, "o—"

"g—"

"g—" He looked up as Tom's broad hand fell sharply on his shoulder. "What you want, fella?"

"What happened—that's what I want to know!"

"Auto hit her. Ins'antly killed."

"Instantly killed," repeated Tom, staring.

"She ran out ina road. Son-of-a-bitch didn't even stopus car."

"There was two cars," said Michaelis. "One comin', one goin', see?"

"Going where?" asked the policeman keenly.

"One goin' each way. Well, she—" His hand rose toward the blankets but stopped halfway and fell to his side, "—she ran out there an' the one comin' from N'York knock right into her goin' thirty or forty miles an hour."

"What's the name of this place here?" demanded the officer.

"Hasn't got any name."

A pale, well-dressed man stepped near.

"It was a yellow car," he said. "Big yellow car. New."

"See the accident?" asked the policeman.

"No, but the car passed me down the road, going faster'n forty. Going fifty, sixty."

"Come here and let's have your name. Look out now. I want to get his name."

Some words of this conversation must have reached Wilson swaying in the office door, for suddenly a new theme found voice among his gasping cries.

"You don't have to tell me what kind of car it was! I know what kind of car it was!"

Watching Tom, I saw the wad of muscle back of his shoulder tighten under his coat. He walked quickly over to Wilson and standing in front of him seized him firmly by the upper arms.

"You've got to pull yourself together," he said with soothing gruffness.

Wilson's eyes fell upon Tom; he started up on his tiptoes and then would have collapsed to his knees had not Tom held him upright.

"Listen," said Tom, shaking him a little. "I just got here a minute ago, from New York. I was bringing you that coupé we've been talking about. That yellow car I was driving this afternoon wasn't mine, do you hear? I haven't seen it all afternoon."

Only I was near enough to hear what he said, but the policeman caught something in the tone and looked over with truculent eyes.

"What's all that?" he demanded.

"I'm a friend of his." Tom turned his head but kept

his hands firm on Wilson's body. "He says he knows the car that did it...It was a yellow car."

Some dim impulse moved the policeman to look suspiciously at Tom.

"And what color's your car?"

"It's a blue car, a coupé."

"We've come straight from New York," Nick said.

Someone who had been driving a little behind us confirmed this and the policeman turned away.

"Now, if you'll let me have that name again correct—"

Picking up Wilson like a doll, Tom carried him into the office, set him down in a chair and came back.

"If somebody'll come here and sit with him!" he snapped authoritatively. He watched while the two men standing closest glanced at each other and went unwillingly into the room. Then Tom shut the door on them and came down the single step, his eyes avoiding the table. As he passed close to Nick, he whispered, "Let's get out."

Self-consciously, with his authoritative arms breaking the way, we pushed through the still gathering crowd, passing a hurried doctor, case in hand, who had been sent for in wild hope half an hour ago.

Tom drove slowly until we were beyond the bend—then his foot came down hard and the coupé raced along through the night. In a little while I heard a low husky sob and saw that the tears were overflowing down his face.

"The God Damn coward!" he whimpered. "He didn't even stop his car."

The Buchanans' house floated suddenly toward us through the dark rustling trees. Tom stopped beside the porch and looked up at the second floor where two windows bloomed with light among the vines.

"Daisy's home," he said. As we got out of the car, he glanced at me and frowned slightly.

"I ought to have dropped you two in West Egg, Nick. There's nothing we can do tonight."

A change had come over him and he spoke gravely, and with decision. As we walked across the moonlight gravel to the porch, he disposed of the situation in a few brisk phrases.

"I'll telephone for a taxi to take you and Dash home, and while you're waiting you and Jordan better go in the kitchen and have them get you some supper —if you want any." He opened the door. "Come in."

"No thanks. But I'd be glad if you'd order me the taxi. I'll wait outside."

Jordan put her hand on Nick's arm.

"Won't you come in, Nick?"

"No thanks."

I was feeling a little sick and I wanted to be alone; I suspect Nick felt the same. But Jordan lingered for a moment more.

"It's only half past nine," she said.

I could tell Nick had had enough of all of them for one day and suddenly that included Jordan as well. She must have seen something of this in his expression, for she turned abruptly away and ran up the porch steps into the house. Nick sat down for a few minutes with his head in his hands. I leaned against him, letting the weight of my body sink into him until we heard the phone taken up inside and the butler's voice calling a taxi.

Then Nick and I walked slowly down the drive away from the house, intending to wait by the gate.

We hadn't gone twenty yards when I heard Nick's name in a whisper and Gatsby stepped from between two bushes into the path. I must have felt pretty weird by that time, because I could think of nothing except the luminosity of his pink suit under the moon.

"What are you doing?" Nick inquired.

"Just standing here, old sport."

Somehow, that seemed a despicable occupation. For all I knew he was going to rob the house in a moment; I wouldn't have been surprised to see sinister faces, the faces of "Wolfsheim's people," behind him in the dark shrubbery.

"Did you see any trouble on the road?" he asked after a minute.

"Yes."

He hesitated.

"Was she killed?"

"Yes."

"I thought so; I told Daisy I thought so. It's better that the shock should all come at once. She stood it pretty well."

He spoke as if Daisy's reaction was the only thing that mattered.

"I got to West Egg by a side road," he went on.

"And left the car in my garage. I don't think anybody saw us, but of course I can't be sure."

I disliked him so much by this time that—even if I had the power of speech—I wouldn't have found it necessary to tell him he was wrong.

"Who was the woman?" he inquired.

"Her name was Wilson. Her husband owns the garage. How the devil did it happen?"

"Well, I tried to swing the wheel—" He broke off, and suddenly I guessed at the truth. Nick did as well.

"Was Daisy driving?"

"Yes," he said after a moment. "But of course I'll say I was. You see, when we left New York, she was very nervous and she thought it would steady her to drive—and this woman rushed out at us just as we were passing a car coming the other way. It all happened in a minute, but it seemed to me that she wanted to speak to us, thought we were somebody she knew. Well, first Daisy turned away from the woman toward the other car, and then she lost her nerve and turned back. The second my hand reached the wheel I felt the shock—it must have killed her instantly."

"It ripped her open—"

"Don't tell me, old sport." He winced. "Anyhow—Daisy stepped on it. I tried to make her stop, but she couldn't, so I pulled on the emergency brake. Then she fell over into my lap and I drove on.

"She'll be all right tomorrow," he said presently. "I'm just going to wait here and see if he tries to bother her about that unpleasantness this afternoon. She's locked herself into her room and if he tries any brutality, she's going to turn the light out and on again."

"He won't touch her," I said. "He's not thinking about her."

"I don't trust him, old sport."

"How long are you going to wait?"

"All night if necessary. Anyhow, till they all go to bed."

A new point of view occurred to me. Suppose Tom found out that Daisy had been driving. He might think he saw a connection in it—he might think anything. I looked at the house: there were two or three bright windows downstairs and the pink glow from Daisy's room on the second floor.

"You wait here," Nick said. "I'll see if there's any sign of a commotion."

Nick and I walked back along the border of the lawn, traversed the gravel softly and tiptoed up the veranda steps, my padded feet making much less sound than his shoes.

The drawing-room curtains were open, and we saw that the room was empty. Crossing the porch where we had dined that June night three months before, we came to a small rectangle of light which I guessed was the pantry window. The blind was drawn, but we found a rift at the sill.

Daisy and Tom were sitting opposite each other at the kitchen table with a plate of cold fried chicken between them and two bottles of ale. He was talking intently across the table at her and in his earnestness his hand had fallen upon and covered her own. Once in a while she looked up at him and nodded in agreement.

They weren't happy, and neither of them had touched the chicken or the ale—and yet they weren't unhappy either. There was an unmistakable air of natural intimacy about the picture and anybody would have said that they were conspiring together.

As we tiptoed from the porch, I heard our taxi feeling its way along the dark road toward the house. Gatsby was waiting where we had left him in the drive.

"Is it all quiet up there?" he asked anxiously.

"Yes, it's all quiet." Nick hesitated. "You'd better come home and get some sleep."

He shook his head.

"I want to wait here till Daisy goes to bed. Good night, old sport. Good night, Dash."

He put his hands in his coat pockets and turned back eagerly to his scrutiny of the house, as though our presence marred the sacredness of the vigil.

So we walked away and left him standing there in the moonlight—watching over nothing.

Chapter Eight

N ick couldn't sleep all night; a foghorn was groaning incessantly on the Sound, and he tossed half-sick between grotesque reality and savage frightening dreams. I lay beside him, sharing the nightmares as best I could. Toward dawn we heard a taxi go up Gatsby's drive and immediately Nick jumped out of bed and began to dress—it was as if Nick felt that he had something to tell him, something to warn him about and morning would be too late.

Crossing his lawn, we saw that his front door was still open and he was leaning against a table in the hall, heavy with dejection or sleep.

"Nothing happened," he said wanly. "I waited, and about four o'clock she came to the window and stood there for a minute and then turned out the light."

His house had never seemed so enormous to me as it did that night when we hunted through the great rooms for cigarettes. They pushed aside curtains that were like pavilions and felt over innumerable feet of dark wall for electric light switches—once Nick tumbled with a sort of splash upon the keys of a ghostly piano. There was an inexplicable amount of dust everywhere and the rooms were musty as though they hadn't been aired for many days. Nick found the humidor on an unfamiliar table with two stale dry cigarettes inside. Throwing open the French windows of the drawing-room, he and Gatsby sat smoking out into the darkness.

"You ought to go away," Nick said. "It's pretty certain they'll trace your car."

"Go away *now*, old sport?"

"Go to Atlantic City for a week, or up to Montreal."

He wouldn't consider it. He couldn't possibly leave Daisy until he knew what she was going to do. He was clutching at some last hope and Nick couldn't bear to shake him free.

It was this night that he told us the strange story of his youth with Dan Cody—told it to us because "Jay Gatsby" had broken up like glass against Tom's hard malice and the long secret extravaganza was played out. I think that he would have acknowledged anything, now, without reserve, but he wanted to talk about Daisy.

She was the first "nice" girl he had ever known. In various unrevealed capacities, he had come in contact with such people, but always with indiscernible barbed wire between. He found her excitingly desirable. He went to her house, at first with other officers from Camp Taylor, then alone. It amazed him—he had never been in such a beautiful house before.

But what gave it an air of breathless intensity was that Daisy lived there—it was as casual a thing to her as his tent out at camp was to him. There was a ripe mystery about it, a hint of bedrooms upstairs more beautiful and cool than other bedrooms, of gay and radiant activities taking place through its corridors and of romances that were not musty and laid away already in lavender, but fresh and breathing and redolent of this year's shining motor cars and of dances whose flowers were scarcely withered. It excited him too that many men had already loved Daisy—it increased her value in his eyes. He felt their presence all about the house, pervading the air with the shades and echoes of still vibrant emotions.

But he knew that he was in Daisy's house by a colossal accident. However glorious might be his future as Jay Gatsby, he was at present a penniless young man without a past, and at any moment the invisible cloak of his uniform might slip from his shoulders. So he made the most of his time. He took what he could get, ravenously and unscrupulously—eventually he took Daisy one still October night, took her because he had no real right to touch her hand.

He might have despised himself, for he had certainly taken her under false pretenses. I don't mean that he had traded on his phantom millions, but he had deliberately given Daisy a sense of security; he let her believe that he was a person from much the same stratum as herself—that he was fully able to take care of her. As a matter of fact, he had no such facilities— he had no comfortable family standing behind him, and he was liable at the whim of an impersonal government to be blown anywhere about the world.

But he didn't despise himself and it didn't turn out as he had imagined. He had intended, probably, to take what he could and go—but now he found that he had committed himself to the following of a grail. He knew that Daisy was extraordinary, but he didn't realize just how extraordinary a "nice" girl could be. She vanished into her rich house, into her rich, full life, leaving Gatsby—nothing. He felt married to her, that was all.

When they met again two days later, it was Gatsby who was breathless, who was somehow betrayed. Her porch was bright with the bought luxury of star-shine; the wicker of the settee squeaked fashionably as she turned toward him, and he kissed her curious and lovely mouth. She had caught a cold and it made her voice huskier and more charming than ever, and Gatsby was overwhelmingly aware of the youth and mystery that wealth imprisons and preserves, of the freshness of many clothes, and of Daisy, gleaming like silver, safe and proud above the hot struggles of the poor.

～

"I can't describe to you how surprised I was to find out I loved her, old sport. I even hoped for a while that she'd throw me over, but she didn't, because she was in love with me too. She thought I knew a lot because I knew different things from her. Well, there I was, way off my ambitions, getting deeper in love every minute, and all of a sudden I didn't care. What was the use of doing great things if I could have a better time telling her what I was going to do?"

On the last afternoon before he went abroad, he sat with Daisy in his arms for a long, silent time. It was a cold fall day with fire in the room and her cheeks flushed. Now and then she moved and he changed his arm a little and once he kissed her dark shining hair. The afternoon had made them tranquil for a while, as if to give them a deep memory for the long parting the next day promised. They had never been closer in their month of love, nor communicated more profoundly one with another, than when she brushed silent lips against his coat's shoulder or when he touched the end of her fingers, gently, as though she were asleep.

He did extraordinarily well in the war. He was a captain before he went to the front, and following the Argonne battles, he got his majority and the command of the divisional machine guns. After the Armistice, he tried frantically to get home, but some complication or misunderstanding sent him to Oxford instead.

He was worried now—there was a quality of nervous despair in Daisy's letters. She didn't see why he couldn't come. She was feeling the pressure of the world outside and she wanted to see him and feel his presence beside her and be reassured that she was doing the right thing after all.

For Daisy was young and her artificial world was redolent of orchids and pleasant, cheerful snobbery and orchestras which set the rhythm of the year, summing up the sadness and suggestiveness of life in new tunes. All night the saxophones wailed the hopeless comment of the "Beale Street Blues," while a hundred pairs of golden and silver slippers shuffled the shining dust. At the grey tea hour there were always rooms that throbbed incessantly with this low sweet fever, while fresh faces drifted here and there like rose petals blown by the sad horns around the floor.

Through this twilight universe, Daisy began to move again with the season; suddenly she was again keeping half a dozen dates a day with half a dozen men and drowsing asleep at dawn with the beads and chiffon of an evening dress tangled among dying orchids on the floor beside her bed. And all the time something within her was crying for a decision. She wanted her life shaped now, immediately—and the decision must be made by some force—of love, of money, of unquestionable practicality—that was close at hand.

That force took shape in the middle of spring with the arrival of Tom Buchanan. There was a wholesome bulkiness about his person and his position and Daisy was flattered. Doubtless there was a certain struggle and a certain relief.

The letter reached Gatsby while he was still at Oxford.

It was dawn now on Long Island, and Gatsby and Nick went about opening the rest of the windows downstairs, filling the house with grey turning, gold turning light. The shadow of a tree fell abruptly across the dew, and ghostly birds began to sing among the blue leaves. There was a slow pleasant movement in the air, scarcely a wind, promising a cool lovely day.

"I don't think she ever loved him." Gatsby turned around from a window and looked at Nick challengingly. "You must remember, old sport, she was very excited this afternoon. He told her those things in a way that frightened her—that made it look as if I was some kind of cheap sharper. And the result was she hardly knew what she was saying."

He sat down gloomily.

"Of course she might have loved him, just for a minute, when they were first married—and loved me more even then, do you see?"

Suddenly he came out with a curious remark:

"In any case," he said, "it was just personal."

What could you make of that, except to suspect some intensity in his conception of the affair that couldn't be measured?

He came back from France when Tom and Daisy were still on their wedding trip, and made a miserable but irresistible journey to Louisville on the last of his army pay. He stayed there a week, walking the streets where their footsteps had clicked together through the November night and revisiting the out-of-the-way places to which they had driven in her white car. Just as Daisy's house had always seemed to him more mysterious and gay than other houses, so his idea of the city itself, even though she was gone from it, was pervaded with a melancholy beauty. He left feeling that if he had searched harder, he might have found her—that he was leaving her behind.

The day-coach—he was penniless now—was hot. He went out to the open vestibule and sat down on a folding-chair, and the station slid away and the backs of unfamiliar buildings moved by. Then out into the spring fields, where a yellow trolley raced them for a minute with people in it who might once have seen the pale magic of her face along the casual street.

The track curved and now it was going away from the sun which, as it sank lower, seemed to spread itself in benediction over the vanishing city where she had drawn her breath. He stretched out his hand desperately, as if to snatch only a wisp of air, to save a fragment of the spot that she had made lovely for him. But it was all going by too fast now for his blurred eyes and he knew that he had lost that part of it, the freshest and the best, forever.

It was nine o'clock when they finished breakfast—including some lovely scraps for me—and went out on the porch. The night had made a sharp difference in the weather and there was an autumn flavor in the air.

The gardener, the last one of Gatsby's former servants, came to the foot of the steps.

"I'm going to drain the pool today, Mr. Gatsby. Leaves will start falling pretty soon and then there's always trouble with the pipes."

"Don't do it today," Gatsby answered. He turned to Nick apologetically. "You know, old sport, I've never used that pool all summer?"

Nick looked at his watch and stood up.

"Twelve minutes to my train."

I know Nick didn't want to go to the city. He wasn't worth a decent stroke of work, but it was more than that—he didn't want to leave Gatsby. Neither did I. Nick missed that train, and then another, before he could get the two of us away.

"I'll call you up," Nick said finally.

"Do, old sport."

"I'll call you about noon."

We walked slowly down the steps.

"I suppose Daisy will call too." He looked at Nick anxiously as if he hoped he'd corroborate this.

"I suppose so."

"Well—goodbye."

They shook hands and Nick and I started away. Just before he reached the hedge, Nick remembered something and turned around.

"They're a rotten crowd," Nick shouted across the lawn. "You're worth the whole damn bunch put together."

I've always been glad he said that and I believe Nick felt the same. It was the only compliment Nick ever gave him, because Nick disapproved of him from beginning to end.

First Gatsby nodded politely, and then his face broke into that radiant and understanding smile, as if we'd been in ecstatic cahoots on that fact all the time. His gorgeous pink rag of a suit made a bright spot of color against the white steps, and I thought of the night when we first came to his ancestral home three months before. The lawn and drive had been crowded with the faces of those who guessed at his corruption—and he had stood on those steps, concealing his incorruptible dream, as he waved them goodbye.

Nick thanked him for his hospitality. People were always thanking him for that—Nick and the others.

"Goodbye," Nick called. "I enjoyed breakfast, Gatsby."

I echoed the sentiment with a single, warm bark.

Up in the city, Nick tried for a while to list the quotations on an interminable amount of stock, then he fell asleep in his swivel-chair, with me napping at his feet. Just before noon the phone woke us both and Nick started up with sweat breaking out on his forehead. It was Jordan Baker; she often called him up at this hour because the uncertainty of her own movements between hotels and clubs and private houses made her hard to find in any other way. Usually her voice came over the wire as something fresh and cool, as if a divot from a green golf links had come sailing in at the office window; but this morning, it seemed harsh and dry.

"I've left Daisy's house," she said. "I'm at Hempstead and I'm going down to Southampton this afternoon."

Probably it had been tactful to leave Daisy's house, but I could tell the act annoyed Nick and her next remark made him rigid.

"You weren't so nice to me last night."

"How could it have mattered then?"

Silence for a moment. Then—

"However—I want to see you."

"I want to see you too."

"Suppose I don't go to Southampton, and come into town this afternoon?"

"No—I don't think this afternoon."

"Very well."

"It's impossible this afternoon. Various—"

They talked like that for a while and then abruptly they weren't talking any longer. I don't know which of them hung up with a sharp click, but I know Nick didn't care. He couldn't have talked to her across a tea-table that day if he never talked to her again in this world. And I felt the same.

Nick called Gatsby's house a few minutes later, but the line was busy. He tried four times; finally, an exasperated central operator told him the wire was being kept open for long distance from Detroit. Taking out the timetable, he drew a small circle around the three-fifty train. Then he leaned back in his chair and tried to think. It was just noon.

When we passed the ash heaps on the train that morning, Nick and I had crossed deliberately to the other side of the car. I suppose there'd be a curious crowd around there all day, with little boys searching for dark spots in the dust and some garrulous man telling over and over what had happened until it became less and less real even to him and he could tell it no longer and Myrtle Wilson's tragic achievement was forgotten.

Now I want to go back a little and tell what happened at the garage after we left there the night before.

They had difficulty in locating the sister, Catherine. She must have broken her rule against drinking that night, for when she arrived, she was stupid with liquor and unable to understand that the ambulance had already gone to Flushing. When they convinced her of this, she immediately fainted, as if that was the intolerable part of the affair. Someone kind or curious took her in his car and drove her in the wake of her sister's body.

Until long after midnight a changing crowd lapped up against the front of the garage, while George Wilson rocked himself back and forth on the couch inside. For a while the door of the office was open and everyone who came into the garage glanced irresistibly through it. Finally, someone said it was a shame and closed the door. Michaelis and several other men were with him—first four or five men, later two or three men. Still later Michaelis had to ask the last stranger to wait there fifteen minutes longer while he went back to his own place and made a pot of coffee. After that, he stayed there alone with Wilson until dawn.

About three o'clock, the quality of Wilson's incoherent muttering changed—he grew quieter and began to talk about the yellow car. He announced that he had a way of finding out whom the yellow car belonged to, and then he blurted out that a couple of months ago his wife had come from the city with her face bruised and her nose swollen.

But when he heard himself say this, he flinched and began to cry "Oh, my God!" again in his groaning voice. Michaelis made a clumsy attempt to distract him.

"How long have you been married, George? Come on there, try and sit still a minute and answer my question. How long have you been married?"

"Twelve years."

"Ever had any children? Come on, George, sit still —I asked you a question. Did you ever have any children?"

The hard brown beetles kept thudding against the dull light, and whenever Michaelis heard a car go tearing along the road outside, it sounded to him like the car that hadn't stopped a few hours before. He didn't like to go into the garage, because the work bench was stained where the body had been lying, so he moved uncomfortably around the office—he knew every object in it before morning—and from time to time sat down beside Wilson, trying to keep him more quiet.

"Have you got a church you go to sometimes, George? Maybe even if you haven't been there for a long time? Maybe I could call up the church and get a priest to come over and he could talk to you, see?"

"Don't belong to any."

"You ought to have a church, George, for times like this. You must have gone to church once. Didn't you get married in a church? Listen, George, listen to me. Didn't you get married in a church?"

"That was a long time ago."

The effort of answering broke the rhythm of his rocking—for a moment he was silent. Then the same half knowing, half bewildered look came back into his faded eyes.

"Look in the drawer there," he said, pointing at the desk.

"Which drawer?"

"That drawer—that one."

Michaelis opened the drawer nearest his hand. There was nothing in it but a small expensive dog leash made of leather and braided silver. It was apparently new.

"This?" he inquired, holding it up.

Wilson stared and nodded.

"I found it yesterday afternoon. She tried to tell me about it, but I knew it was something funny."

"You mean your wife bought it?"

"She had it wrapped in tissue paper on her bureau."

Michaelis didn't see anything odd in that and he gave Wilson a dozen reasons why his wife might have bought the dog leash. But conceivably Wilson had heard some of these same explanations before, from Myrtle, because he began saying "Oh, my God!" again in a whisper—his comforter left several explanations in the air.

"Then he killed her," said Wilson. His mouth dropped open suddenly.

"Who did?"

"I have a way of finding out."

"You're morbid, George," said his friend. "This has been a strain to you, and you don't know what you're saying. You'd better try and sit quiet till morning."

"He murdered her."

"It was an accident, George."

Wilson shook his head. His eyes narrowed and his mouth widened slightly with the ghost of a superior "Hm!"

"I know," he said definitely. "I'm one of these trusting fellas and I don't think any harm to *no*body, but when I get to know a thing, I know it. It was the man in that car. She ran out to speak to him and he wouldn't stop."

Michaelis had seen this too, but it hadn't occurred to him that there was any special significance in it. He believed that Mrs. Wilson had been running away from her husband, rather than trying to stop any particular car.

"How could she have been like that?"

"She's a deep one," said Wilson, as if that answered the question. "Ah-h-h—"

He began to rock again and Michaelis stood twisting the leash in his hand.

"Maybe you got some friend that I could telephone for, George?"

This was a forlorn hope—he was almost sure that Wilson had no friend: there was not enough of him for his wife. He was glad a little later when he noticed a change in the room, a blue quickening by the window, and realized that dawn wasn't far off. About five o'clock it was blue enough outside to snap off the light.

Wilson's glazed eyes turned out to the ash heaps, where small grey clouds took on fantastic shapes and scurried here and there in the faint dawn wind.

"I spoke to her," he muttered, after a long silence. "I told her she might fool me but she couldn't fool God. I took her to the window—" With an effort he got up and walked to the rear window and leaned with his face pressed against it. "—and I said 'God knows what you've been doing, everything you've been doing. You may fool me but you can't fool God!'"

Standing behind him, Michaelis saw with a shock that he was looking at the eyes of Doctor T. J. Eckleburg which had just emerged pale and enormous from the dissolving night.

"God sees everything," repeated Wilson.

"That's an advertisement," Michaelis assured him. Something made him turn away from the window and look back into the room. But Wilson stood there a long time, his face close to the windowpane, nodding into the twilight.

By six o'clock Michaelis was worn out and grateful for the sound of a car stopping outside. It was one of the watchers of the night before who had promised to come back, so he cooked breakfast for three, which he and the other man ate together. Wilson was quieter now and Michaelis went home to sleep; when he awoke four hours later and hurried back to the garage, Wilson was gone.

His movements—he was on foot all the time—were afterward traced to Port Roosevelt and then to Gad's Hill, where he bought a sandwich that he didn't eat and a cup of coffee. He must have been tired and walking slowly, for he didn't reach Gad's Hill until noon. Thus far there was no difficulty in accounting for his time—there were boys who had seen a man "acting sort of crazy" and motorists at whom he stared oddly from the side of the road.

Then for three hours, he disappeared from view. The police, on the strength of what he said to Michaelis, that he "had a way of finding out," supposed that he spent that time going from garage to garage thereabouts inquiring for a yellow car. On the other hand, no garage man who had seen him ever came forward—and perhaps he had an easier, surer way of finding out what he wanted to know.

By half past two he was in West Egg, where he

asked someone the way to Gatsby's house. So, by that time, he knew Gatsby's name.

At two o'clock, Gatsby put on his bathing suit and left word with the butler that if any one phoned, word was to be brought to him at the pool. He stopped at the garage for a pneumatic mattress that had amused his guests during the summer, and the chauffeur helped him pump it up. Then he gave instructions that the open car wasn't to be taken out under any circumstances—and this was strange because the front right fender needed repair.

Gatsby shouldered the mattress and started for the pool. Once he stopped and shifted it a little, and the chauffeur asked him if he needed help, but he shook his head and in a moment disappeared among the yellowing trees.

No telephone message arrived, but the butler went without his sleep and waited for it until four o'clock—until long after there was any one to give it to if it came. I have an idea that Gatsby himself didn't believe it would come and perhaps he no longer cared. If that was true, he must have felt that he had lost the old warm world, paid a high price for living too long with a single dream. He must have looked up at an unfamiliar sky through frightening leaves and shivered as he found what a grotesque thing a rose is and how raw the sunlight was upon the scarcely created grass. A new world, material without being real, where poor ghosts, breathing dreams like air, drifted fortuitously about...like that ashen, fantastic figure gliding toward him through the amorphous trees.

The chauffeur—he was one of Wolfsheim's protégés—heard the shots—afterward he could only say that he hadn't thought anything much about them. Nick and I drove from the station directly to Gatsby's house and our rushing anxiously up the front steps was the first thing that alarmed anyone. But they knew then, I firmly believe. With scarcely a word said, five of us—the chauffeur, butler, gardener, Nick and I—hurried down to the pool.

There was a faint, barely perceptible movement of the water as the fresh flow from one end urged its way toward the drain at the other. With little ripples that were hardly the shadows of waves, the laden mattress moved irregularly down the pool. A small gust of wind that scarcely corrugated the surface was enough to disturb its accidental course with its accidental burden. The touch of a cluster of leaves revolved it slowly, tracing, like the leg of a compass, a thin red circle in the water.

It was after we started with Gatsby toward the house that the gardener saw Wilson's body a little way off in the grass, and the holocaust was complete.

Chapter Nine

After two years, I remember the rest of that day, and that night and the next day, only as an endless drill of police and photographers and newspaper men in and out of Gatsby's front door. A rope stretched across the main gate and a policeman by it kept out the curious, but little boys soon discovered that they could enter through our yard and there were always a few of them clustered open-mouthed about the pool.

Someone with a positive manner, perhaps a detective, used the expression "mad man" as he bent over Wilson's body that afternoon, and the adventitious authority of his voice set the key for the newspaper reports next morning.

Most of those reports were a nightmare—grotesque, circumstantial, eager and untrue. When Michaelis's testimony at the inquest brought to light Wilson's suspicions of his wife, I thought the whole tale would shortly be served up in racy pasquinade—but Catherine, who might have said anything, didn't say a word. She showed a surprising amount of character about it too—looked at the coroner with determined eyes under that corrected brow of hers and swore that her sister had never seen Gatsby, that her sister was completely happy with her husband, that her sister had been into no mischief whatsoever.

She convinced herself of it and cried into her handkerchief as if the very suggestion was more than she could endure. So Wilson was reduced to a man "deranged by grief" in order that the case might remain in its simplest form. And it rested there.

But all this part of it seemed remote and unessential. Nick and I found ourselves on Gatsby's side, and alone. From the moment Nick telephoned news of the catastrophe to West Egg village, every surmise about him, and every practical question, was referred to Nick.

At first, Nick was surprised and confused; then, as he lay in his house and didn't move or breathe or speak hour upon hour, it grew upon Nick that he was responsible, because no one else was interested—interested, I mean, with that intense personal interest to which everyone has some vague right at the end.

Nick called up Daisy half an hour after we found him, called her instinctively and without hesitation. But she and Tom had gone away early that afternoon and taken baggage with them.

"Left no address?"

"No."

"Say when they'd be back?"

"No."

"Any idea where they are? How I could reach them?"

"I don't know. Can't say."

I could tell Nick wanted to get somebody for Gatsby. He wanted to go into the room where he lay and reassure him: "I'll get somebody for you, Gatsby. Don't worry. Just trust me and I'll get somebody for you—"

Meyer Wolfsheim's name wasn't in the phone book. The butler gave Nick his office address on Broadway and Nick called Information, but by the time he had the number, it was long after five and no one answered the phone.

"Will you ring again?"

"I've rung them three times."

"It's very important."

"Sorry. I'm afraid no one's there."

Nick and I went back to the drawing room and I thought for an instant that they were chance visitors, all these official people who suddenly filled it. But as they drew back the sheet and looked at Gatsby with unmoved eyes, his protest continued in my brain and I'm sure in Nick's as well.

"Look here, old sport, you've got to get somebody for me. You've got to try hard. I can't go through this alone."

Someone started to ask Nick questions, but he broke away and, going upstairs, he looked hastily through the unlocked parts of Gatsby's desk—he'd never told us definitely that his parents were dead. But there was nothing—only the picture of Dan Cody, a token of forgotten violence staring down from the wall.

Next morning Nick sent the butler to New York with a letter to Wolfsheim, which asked for information and urged him to come out on the next train. That request seemed superfluous when he wrote it. We were both sure he'd start when he saw the newspapers, just as we were sure there'd be a wire from Daisy before noon—but neither a wire nor Mr. Wolfsheim arrived, no one arrived except more police and photographers and newspaper men.

When the butler brought back Wolfsheim's answer, Nick and I began to have a feeling of defiance, of scornful solidarity among Gatsby and me and Nick against them all.

Nick read the letter aloud, as much for himself as for me, I think.

Dear Mr. Carraway.

This has been one of the most terrible shocks of my life to me. I hardly can believe it that it is true at all. Such a mad act as that man did should make us all think. I cannot come down now as I am tied up in some very important business and cannot get mixed up in this thing now. If there is anything I can do a little later let me know in a letter by Edgar. I hardly know where I am when I hear about a thing like this and am completely knocked down and out.

Yours truly,
MEYER WOLFSHIEM

and then hasty addenda beneath:

Let me know about the funeral etc., do not know his family at all.

When the phone rang that afternoon and Long Distance said Chicago was calling, we thought this would be Daisy at last. But the connection came through as a man's voice, very thin and far away.

"This is Slagle speaking..."

"Yes?" The name was unfamiliar.

"Hell of a note, isn't it? Get my wire?"

"There haven't been any wires."

"Young Parke's in trouble," he said rapidly. "They picked him up when he handed the bonds over the counter. They got a circular from New York giving 'em the numbers just five minutes before. What d' you know about that, hey? You never can tell in these hick towns—"

"Hello!" Nick interrupted breathlessly. "Look here —this isn't Mr. Gatsby. Mr. Gatsby's dead."

There was a long silence on the other end of the wire, followed by an exclamation ... then a quick squawk as the connection was broken.

I think it was on the third day that a telegram signed Henry C. Gatz arrived from a town in Minnesota. It said only that the sender was leaving immediately and to postpone the funeral until he came.

It was Gatsby's father, a solemn old man very helpless and dismayed, bundled up in a long cheap ulster against the warm September day. His eyes leaked continuously with excitement and when Nick took the bag and umbrella from his hands, he began to pull so incessantly at his sparse grey beard that Nick had difficulty in getting off his coat. He was on the point of collapse, so Nick took him into the music room and made him sit down while he sent for something to eat. But he wouldn't eat, and the glass of milk spilled from his trembling hand.

"I saw it in the Chicago newspaper," he said. "It was all in the Chicago newspaper. I started right away."

"I didn't know how to reach you."

His eyes, seeing nothing, moved ceaselessly about the room.

"It was a mad man," he said. "He must have been mad."

"Wouldn't you like some coffee?" Nick urged him.

"I don't want anything. I'm all right now, Mr.—"

"Carraway."

"Well, I'm all right now. Where have they got Jimmy?"

Nick took him into the drawing-room, where his son lay, and left him there. Some little boys had come up on the steps and were looking into the hall; when Nick told them who had arrived, they went reluctantly away.

After a little while, Mr. Gatz opened the door and came out, his mouth ajar, his face flushed slightly, his eyes leaking isolated and unpunctual tears. He had reached an age where death no longer has the quality of ghastly surprise, and when he looked around him now for the first time and saw the height and splendor of the hall and the great rooms opening out from it into other rooms, his grief began to be mixed with an awed pride.

Nick helped him to a bedroom upstairs; while he took off his coat and vest, Nick told him that all arrangements had been deferred until he came.

"I didn't know what you'd want, Mr. Gatsby—"

"Gatz is my name."

"—Mr. Gatz. I thought you might want to take the body west."

He shook his head.

"Jimmy always liked it better down East. He rose up to his position in the East. Were you a friend of my boy's, Mr.—?"

"We were close friends."

"He had a big future before him, you know. He was only a young man, but he had a lot of brain power here."

He touched his head impressively and Nick nodded.

"If he'd of lived he'd of been a great man. A man like James J. Hill. He'd of helped build up the country."

"That's true," Nick said, uncomfortably.

He fumbled at the embroidered coverlet, trying to

take it from the bed, and lay down stiffly—and was instantly asleep.

~

That night an obviously frightened person called up and demanded to know who Nick was before he would give his name.

"This is Mr. Carraway," Nick said.

"Oh—" He sounded relieved. "This is Klipspringer."

I was relieved—and Nick as well—for that seemed to promise another friend at Gatsby's grave. We didn't want it to be in the papers and draw a sightseeing crowd, so Nick had been calling up a few people himself. They were hard to find.

"The funeral's tomorrow," Nick said. "Three o'clock, here at the house. I wish you'd tell anybody who'd be interested."

"Oh, I will," he broke out hastily. "Of course, I'm not likely to see anybody, but if I do."

His tone made us suspicious.

"Of course, you'll be there yourself."

"Well, I'll certainly try. What I called up about is—"

"Wait a minute," Nick interrupted. "How about saying you'll come?"

"Well, the fact is—the truth of the matter is that I'm staying with some people up here in Greenwich and they rather expect me to be with them tomorrow.

In fact, there's a sort of picnic or something. Of course, I'll do my very best to get away."

Nick ejaculated an unrestrained "Huh!" and the man must have heard him, for he went on nervously:

"What I called up about was a pair of shoes I left there. I wonder if it'd be too much trouble to have the butler send them on. You see they're tennis shoes and I'm sort of helpless without them. My address is care of B. F.—"

I didn't hear the rest of the name, because Nick hung up the receiver.

The morning of the funeral, we went up to New York to see Meyer Wolfsheim; Nick couldn't seem to reach him any other way. The door that he pushed open on the advice of an elevator boy was marked "The Swastika Holding Company" and at first there didn't seem to be any one inside. But when he'd shouted "Hello" several times in vain, an argument broke out behind a partition, and presently a lovely woman appeared at an interior door and scrutinized us with black hostile eyes.

"Nobody's in," she said. "Mr. Wolfsheim's gone to Chicago."

The first part of this was obviously untrue for someone had begun to whistle "The Rosary," tunelessly, inside.

"Please say that Mr. Carraway wants to see him."

"I can't get him back from Chicago, can I?"

At this moment a voice, unmistakably Wolfsheim's called "Stella!" from the other side of the door.

"Leave your name on the desk," she said quickly. "I'll give it to him when he gets back."

"But I know he's there."

She took a step toward me and began to slide her hands indignantly up and down her hips.

"You young men think you can force your way in here any time," she scolded. "We're getting sick and tired of it. When I say he's in Chicago, he's in Chicago."

Nick mentioned Gatsby.

"Oh—h!" She looked at us again. "Will you just— what was your name?"

She vanished. In a moment, Meyer Wolfsheim stood solemnly in the doorway, holding out both hands. He drew us into his office, remarking in a reverent voice that it was a sad time for all of us, and offered Nick a cigar. He apologized to me for not having any biscuits handy.

"My memory goes back to when I first met him," he said. "A young major just out of the army and covered over with medals he got in the war. He was so hard up, he had to keep on wearing his uniform because he couldn't buy some regular clothes. First time I saw him was when he come into Winebrenner's poolroom at Forty-third Street and asked for a job. He hadn't eaten anything for a couple of days. 'Come on have some lunch with me,' I said. He ate more than four dollars' worth of food in half an hour."

"Did you start him in business?" Nick inquired.

"Start him! I made him."

"Oh."

"I raised him up out of nothing, right out of the gutter. I saw right away he was a fine appearing, gentlemanly young man, and when he told me he was an Oggsford, I knew I could use him good. I got him to join up in the American Legion and he used to stand high there. Right off he did some work for a client of mine up to Albany. We were so thick like that in every-thing—" He held up two bulbous fingers "—always together."

I could tell Nick wondered if this partnership had included the World's Series transaction in 1919; it was a question I held as well.

"Now he's dead," Nick said after a moment. "You were his closest friend, so I know you'll want to come to his funeral this afternoon."

"I'd like to come."

"Well, come then."

The hair in his nostrils quivered slightly and as he shook his head his eyes filled with tears.

"I can't do it—I can't get mixed up in it," he said.

"There's nothing to get mixed up in. It's all over now."

"When a man gets killed, I never like to get mixed up in it in any way. I keep out. When I was a young man it was different—if a friend of mine died, no matter how, I stuck with them to the end. You may think that's sentimental, but I mean it—to the bitter end."

Nick saw that for some reason of his own he was

determined not to come, so he stood up. I rose to my four feet as well.

He shook Nick's hand and patted my head warmly.

"Let us learn to show our friendship for a man when he is alive and not after he is dead," he suggested. "After that, my own rule is to let everything alone."

When we left his office, the sky had turned dark and we got back to West Egg in a drizzle. After Nick changed his clothes, we went next door and found Mr. Gatz walking up and down excitedly in the hall. His pride in his son and in his son's possessions was continually increasing and now he had something to show us.

"Jimmy sent me this picture." He took out his wallet with trembling fingers. "Look there."

It was a photograph of the house, cracked in the corners and dirty with many hands. He pointed out every detail to us eagerly. "Look there!" and then sought admiration from first Nick's eyes and then mine. He had shown it so often that I think it was more real to him now than the house itself.

"Jimmy sent it to me. I think it's a very pretty picture. It shows up well."

"Very well. Had you seen him lately?"

"He come out to see me two years ago and bought me the house I live in now. Of course, we was broke up when he run off from home, but I see now there was a reason for it. He knew he had a big future in front of him. And ever since he made a success, he was very generous with me."

He seemed reluctant to put away the picture, held

it for another minute, lingeringly, before our eyes. Then he returned the wallet and pulled from his pocket a ragged old copy of a book called "Hopalong Cassidy."

"Look here, this is a book he had when he was a boy. It just shows you."

He opened it at the back cover and turned it around for us to see.

On the last flyleaf was printed the word SCHEDULE, and the date September 12th, 1906. And underneath:

SCHEDULE

    Rise from bed 6.00 A.M.
    Dumbbell exercise and wall-scaling. 6.15-6.30
    Study electricity, etc. 7.15-8.15
    Work. 8.30-4.30 P.M.
    Baseball and sports. 4.30-5.00
    Practice elocution, poise and how to attain it. 5.00-6.00
    Study needed inventions. 7.00-9.00

GENERAL RESOLVES

    No wasting time at Shafters or [a name, indecipherable]
    No more smokeing or chewing
    Bath every other day
    Read one improving book or magazine per week
    Save $5.00 [crossed out] $3.00 per week
    Be better to parents

"I come across this book by accident," said the old man. "It just shows you, don't it?"

"It just shows you."

"Jimmy was bound to get ahead. He always had some resolves like this or something. Do you notice what he's got about improving his mind? He was always great for that. He told me I ate like a hog once and I beat him for it."

He was reluctant to close the book, reading each item aloud and then looking eagerly at us. I think he rather expected Nick to copy down the list for his own use.

A little before three, the Lutheran minister arrived from Flushing and I began to look involuntarily out the windows for other cars. So did Nick and Gatsby's father. And as the time passed and the servants came in and stood waiting in the hall, Gatsby's father eyes began to blink anxiously and he spoke of the rain in a worried uncertain way.

The minister glanced several times at his watch, so Nick took him aside and asked him to wait for half an hour. But it wasn't any use. Nobody came.

About five o'clock, our procession of three cars reached the cemetery and stopped in a thick drizzle beside the gate—first a motor hearse, horribly black and wet, then Mr. Gatz and the minister and Nick and I in the limousine, and, a little later, four or five servants and the postman from West Egg in Gatsby's station wagon, all wet to the skin.

As we started through the gate into the cemetery, I heard a car stop and then the sound of someone splashing after us over the soggy ground. I looked around. It was the man with owl-eyed glasses whom Nick and I had found marveling over Gatsby's books in the library one night three months before.

I'd never seen him since then. I don't know how he knew about the funeral or even his name. The rain poured down his thick glasses and he took them off and wiped them to see the protecting canvas unrolled from Gatsby's grave.

I tried to think about Gatsby then for a moment, but he was already too far away and I could only remember, without resentment, that Daisy hadn't sent a message or a flower. Dimly I heard someone murmur "Blessed are the dead that the rain falls on," and then the owl-eyed man said, "Amen to that," in a brave voice.

We straggled down quickly through the rain to the cars. Owl-Eyes spoke to Nick by the gate.

"I couldn't get to the house," he remarked.

"Neither could anybody else."

"Go on!" He started. "Why, my God! They used to go there by the hundreds."

He took off his glasses and wiped them again outside and in.

"The poor son-of-a-bitch," he said.

After Gatsby's death, the East felt haunted for us. So, when the blue smoke of brittle leaves was in the air and the wind blew the wet laundry stiff on the line, Nick decided to come back home and I agreed. It was time.

There was one thing to be done before we left, an awkward, unpleasant thing that perhaps had better have been let alone. But Nick wanted to leave things in order and not just trust that obliging and indifferent sea to sweep his refuse away. He saw Jordan Baker and talked over and around what had happened to them together and what had happened afterward to Nick, and she lay perfectly still listening in a big chair.

She was dressed to play golf and I remember thinking she looked like a good illustration, her chin raised a little, jauntily, her hair the color of an autumn leaf, her face the same brown tint as the fingerless glove on her knee. When Nick had finished, she told him without comment that she was engaged to another man. I doubted that, though there were several she could have married at a nod of her head, but Nick pretended to be surprised. For just a minute I think he wondered if he wasn't making a mistake, then he thought it all over again quickly and got up to say goodbye. I was already on my feet.

"Nevertheless, you did throw me over," said Jordan suddenly. "You threw me over on the telephone. I don't give a damn about you now, but it was a new experience for me and I felt a little dizzy for a while."

They shook hands. As she had done so often in the

past, Jordan went out of her way to ignore me. Like there was no reason for a dog to be a part of her story.

"Oh, and do you remember—" she added, "—a conversation we had once about driving a car?"

"Why—not exactly."

"You said a bad driver was only safe until she met another bad driver? Well, I met another bad driver, didn't I? I mean it was careless of me to make such a wrong guess. I thought you were rather an honest, straightforward person. I thought it was your secret pride."

"I'm thirty," Nick said. "I'm five years too old to lie to myself and call it honor."

She didn't answer. Angry, and half in love with her, and tremendously sorry, Nick turned away. I was already halfway to the door.

One afternoon late in October, we saw Tom Buchanan. He was walking ahead of us along Fifth Avenue in his alert, aggressive way, his hands out a little from his body as if to fight off interference, his head moving sharply here and there, adapting itself to his restless eyes. I've raced dogs like that. They often won, just by the sheer force of their will, with little regard to their actual skill.

Just as we slowed up to avoid overtaking him, he stopped and began frowning into the windows of a jewelry store. Suddenly he saw us and walked back holding out his hand.

"What's the matter, Nick? Do you object to shaking hands with me?"

"Yes. You know what I think of you."

"You're crazy, Nick," he said quickly. "Crazy as hell. I don't know what's the matter with you."

"Tom," Nick inquired, "what did you say to Wilson that afternoon?"

He stared at us without a word and I knew I had guessed right about those missing hours. Nick started to turn away, but he took a step after him and grabbed his arm.

"I told him the truth," he said. "He came to the door while we were getting ready to leave, and when I sent down word that we weren't in, he tried to force his way upstairs. He was crazy enough to kill me if I hadn't told him who owned the car. His hand was on a revolver in his pocket every minute he was in the house —" He broke off defiantly. "What if I did tell him? That fellow had it coming to him. He threw dust into your eyes just like he did in Daisy's, but he was a tough one. He ran over Myrtle like you'd run over a dog and never even stopped his car."

I winced at the expression, which I felt sure had not been accidental. He didn't like Nick and he didn't like me.

There was nothing Nick could say, except the one unutterable fact that it wasn't true.

"And if you think I didn't have my share of suffering—look here, when I went to give up that flat and saw that damn box of dog biscuits sitting there on the sideboard, I sat down and cried like a baby. By God it was awful—"

I was momentarily confused by the food reference, and then remembered the entire, drunken scenario. A baffling afternoon with the humans, all boozy and drunk.

I couldn't forgive him or like him—and I know Nick felt the same—but I saw that what he had done was, to him, entirely justified. It was all very careless and confused. They were careless people, Tom and Daisy—they smashed up things and creatures and then retreated back into their money or their vast carelessness or whatever it was that kept them together, and let other people clean up the mess they had made...

Nick shook hands with him; it seemed silly not to, for it felt suddenly as though we were talking to a child. Then he went into the jewelry store to buy a pearl necklace—or perhaps only a pair of cuff buttons—rid of our provincial squeamishness forever.

Gatsby's house was still empty when we left—the grass on his lawn had grown as long as ours. One of the taxi drivers in the village never took a fare past the entrance gate without stopping for a minute and pointing inside; perhaps it was he who drove Daisy and Gatsby over to East Egg the night of the accident and perhaps he had made a story about it all his own. We didn't want to hear it and Nick and I avoided him when I got off the train.

We spent our Saturday nights in New York, because those gleaming, dazzling parties of his were with us so vividly that we could still hear the music and the laughter faint and incessant from his garden and the cars going up and down his drive. One night I did hear a material car there and saw its lights stop at his front steps. But I didn't investigate. Probably it was some final guest who had been away at the ends of the earth and didn't know that the party was over.

On the last night, with Nick's trunk packed and his car sold to the grocer, we went over and looked at that huge incoherent failure of a house once more. On the white steps an obscene word, scrawled by some boy with a piece of brick, stood out clearly in the moonlight. Nick erased it, drawing his shoe raspingly along the stone. Then we wandered down to the beach and sprawled out on the sand.

Most of the big shore places were closed now and there were hardly any lights except the shadowy, moving glow of a ferryboat across the Sound. And as the moon rose higher, the inessential houses began to melt away until gradually I became aware of the old island here that flowered once for Dutch sailors' eyes— a fresh, green breast of the new world. Its vanished trees, the trees that had made way for Gatsby's house, had once pandered in whispers to the last and greatest of all human dreams; for a transitory enchanted moment, man must have held his breath in the presence of this continent, compelled into an aesthetic contemplation he neither understood nor desired, face to face for the last time in history with something commensurate to his capacity for wonder.

And as we sat there brooding on the old, unknown world, I thought of Gatsby's wonder when he first picked out the green light at the end of Daisy's dock. He had come a long way to this blue lawn and his dream must have seemed so close that he could hardly fail to grasp it. He did not know that it was already behind him, somewhere back in that vast obscurity beyond the city, where the dark fields of the republic rolled on under the night.

Gatsby believed in the green light, the orgiastic future that year by year recedes before us. It eluded us then, but that's no matter—tomorrow we will run faster, stretch out our legs farther...And one fine morning—

And so we beat on, boats against the current, borne back ceaselessly into the past.

The Greyhound of the Baskervilles

A new take on the Arthur Conan Doyle's classic mystery, "The Hound of the Baskervilles."

Think you know this story? Well, you haven't experienced it until you've read it through the eyes of Sherlock's pet dog.

It's the classic tale, now narrated by a dog. A greyhound, in fact, named Septimus.

Holmes and Watson ... and Septimus ... are called to the Baskerville estate to protect the new Baron and see if there is any truth to the legend of the hound of the Baskervilles. It's a dog-meet-dog mystery as Septimus sniffs out the clues, detects the red herrings and goes head-to-head with the monsterous creature which is haunting the moors.

It's the classic you love ... but now it's a slightly different tail!

"A delightful tale, familiar and yet filled with surprises."

Grab it now!

★★★★★

https://www.albertsbridgebooks.com

A Christmas Carl

A CHRISTMAS CARL
A Greyhound Ghost Story of Christmas

A delightful new take on the Charles Dickens' classic story, "A Christmas Carol."

Think you know this story? Well, you haven't

experienced "A Christmas Carol" until you've read it through the eyes of Scrooge's pet dog.

It's the classic tale you know, now narrated by a dog. A greyhound named Carl.

Ebenezer Scrooge—and his faithful greyhound, Carl—are visited on Christmas Eve by the ghost of his dead partner, Jacob Marley. What follows is the story you know, but with a twist. With faithful Carl by his side, Scrooge experiences the Ghosts of Christmas Past, Present and Future, taking away a lesson that will forever change his—and Carl's—life forever.

It's the classic you love ... but now it's a slightly different tail!

Grab it today!
https://www.albertsbridgebooks.com

Join The Newsletter

Keep in touch about all the books at Albert's Bridge books — The Como Lake Players mysteries ... the Eli Marks mysteries ... plus occasional deals on other mysteries! And no spam!

Click HERE to join!

Get Your Free Eli Marks Short Story Bundle

**The Eli Marks Short Mystery Bundle
"The Invisible Assistant" & "The Last Customer"**

Two short-story cozy mysteries in one!

"You will just LOVE these books." VANISH Magazine

The Invisible Assistant

There's no question it was murder. But who killed whom?

What begins as a typical corporate event for magician Eli Marks turns into a twisted mystery when he is called to the site of a recent murder/suicide. Confronted by the details of the grisly crime scene, Eli must sort through the post-mortem clues - and the bickering of the officials as well as a poorly-timed allergy attack - to determine just who murdered whom.

The Last Customer

The request was a first for Eli Marks: "Can you help me make my tuba disappear?"

Magician (and magic shop owner) Eli Marks is confronted with this odd demand just before he is about to close up shop for the day. Over the next few tense minutes, he finds a solution to that question which also, fortunately, puts him the positive side of what turns out to be a life-or-death situation.

Click HERE to grab your free copy!

Or go to www.elimarksmysteries.com

F. Scott Fitzgerald is the acclaimed author of "The Great Gatsby" and a pillar of American literature. He penned four other novels, including "Tender is the Night" and "This Side of Paradise," as well as numerous short stories, imbued with his distinctive blend of romanticism and keen social insight.

Fitzgerald is known as the poster boy of the "Roaring Twenties," with his writing capturing the spirit, excess, and disillusionment of the era. His works remain relevant today, universally recognized for their profound exploration of the American Dream.

In addition to his novels, Fitzgerald also dabbled in playwriting and screenwriting, bringing his poignant storytelling to the stage and screen. His personal life was as tumultuous and fascinating as his fiction, marked by his tumultuous relationship with his wife, Zelda, and his struggles with alcoholism.

Fitzgerald spent his last years in Hollywood and died at the age of 44, leaving behind a lasting legacy in American literature. He continues to inspire writers and readers around the world.

About the Other Author

John is author of the Eli Marks mystery series and the Como Lake Players mystery series. He also has five other stand-alone novels, including several greyhound inspired pastiches, including this volume, as well as "The Greyhound of the Baskervilles" and "A Christmas Carl."

John has directed six low-budget features and has written multiple books on the subject of low-budget filmmaking. In addition, he wrote two craft books for novelists: "The Popcorn Principles" and "More Popcorn Principles: The Sequel."

His most recent fiction book is the ninth book in his Eli Marks series ("The Professor's Nightmare") as well as a prequel to the Eli Marks series, "The Curious Mysteries of Eli Marks." The Middle Grade book introduces us to thirteen-year-old Eli and explores how he came to the world of magic and magicians.

He lives in Minneapolis and shares his home with his lovely wife, two greyhounds, a couple cats and a handful of pet allergies.

Books By John Gaspard

The Como Lake Players Mysteries
ACTING CAN BE MURDER
DYING TO AUDITION
REHEARSED TO DEATH
AN OPENING NIGHTMARE (Novella)

The Eli Marks Mystery Series
THE AMBITIOUS CARD (#1)
THE BULLET CATCH (#2)
THE MISER'S DREAM (#3)
THE LINKING RINGS (#4)
THE FLOATING LIGHT BULB (#5)
THE ZOMBIE BALL (#6)
THE MAGIC SQUARE (#7)
THE SELF-WORKING TRICK (#8)
THE PROFESSOR'S NIGHTMARE (#9)

The Young Eli Marks Mystery Series

THE CURIOUS MYSTERIES OF ELI
MARKS (#1)

Stand-Alone Novels
THE SWORD & MR. STONE
A CHRISTMAS CARL
THE GREYHOUND OF THE BASKERVILLES
THE GREYHOUND & GATSBY
THE RIPPEROLOGISTS

Filmmaking/Writing Books
THE POPCORN PRINCIPLES
MORE POPCORN PRINCIPLES: THE SEQUEL!
FAST, CHEAP AND UNDER CONTROL
FAST, CHEAP AND WRITTEN THAT WAY
TELL THEM IT'S A DREAM SEQUENCE
WOMEN MAKE MOVIES

www.ingramcontent.com/pod-product-compliance
Lightning Source LLC
Chambersburg PA
CBHW072124300726

48975CB00003B/915